FIRST MAN
What's wrong with him?

WOMAN
He was bit by a dog. Nasty place he's got.

FIRST MAN
Did you have it cauterised? They're nasty things, dog-bites.

WOMAN
Oh, yes, we had it cauterised, you may be sure.

SECOND MAN [Reflectively]
Dangerous things, dogs.

FIRST MAN
If they're not properly looked after, they are. Now I've got a little dog....

[At this point the speaker's voice becomes inaudible owing to the passing of the brontosauri, which gradually move off L.

WOMAN [Becoming audible and apparently interrupting in the middle of an anecdote]
Though I tell Johnnie it's his own fault. He shouldn't have teased him.

[Enter R. a few thousand savages with flat weapons.

SECOND MAN
Boys will be boys.

WOMAN
Which is no reason, I say, that they shouldn't learn to behave themselves.

FIRST MAN
Can't begin too soon, in my opinion.

[Exeunt savages: enter the population of India.

WOMAN
He might have been killed if a man hadn't come up and pulled the dog off him. A black man, he was, too.

FIRST MAN
What? A nigger?

WOMAN
Or a Turk, or something. I can't never see the difference. [With a shiver.] Ugh! I hate black men, somehow. The look of 'em gives me the shudders.

SECOND MAN [On a note of faint expostulation]

My dear!

FIRST MAN
I've heard others say the same thing.

WOMAN
A pretty penny, Johnnie'll cost us, with the Doctor and all.

[Enter two armies engaged in a Civil War.

FIRST MAN [Shaking his head, wisely]
Ah! I daresay it will.

SECOND MAN
I don't know what we're coming to, what with wages and prices and Lord knows what all?

FIRST MAN
No more do I. Why, only yesterday....

[The rest of his sentence is drowned by the firing of a battery of heavy guns.

WOMAN
Oh! well, I suppose it'll all come right in time.

[The Civil War moves off L. Signs of the approaching end of the world become manifest.

FIRST MAN
We'll hope for the best, I'm sure.

[The Hosts of Heaven appear in the sky.

SECOND MAN [Reflectively]
On the whole, I should say that things looked a bit better than they did.

[The Sea gives up its Dead.

WOMAN
We shall take Johnnie to Ramsgate, as soon as his arm's well.

FIRST MAN
We always go to Scarborough.

SECOND MAN
We have to consider the expense of the journey, especially now there's no cheap trains.

[The universe bursts into flame. For a moment all is confusion; and then the Spirit of the First Man is heard speaking.

Signs & Wonders by John Davys Beresford

John Davys Beresford was born on the 17th March 1873.

His early life was blighted by infantile paralysis which left him with lasting physical challenges.

After being educated at Oundle School he trained to become an architect. This gave way to his literary ambitions, first as a dramatist and then into journalism.

His father, a clergyman, was disappointed that his son moved to become, as he put it; 'a determined but defensive' agnostic, though in later years his views would change again and he would declare himself a Theosophist and a pacifist.

Beresford contributed book reviews to The Manchester Guardian, as well as writing for the New Statesman, The Spectator, Westminster Gazette, and The Aryan Path, the Theosophist magazine.

Although offered the editorship of the latter he declined thinking he did not have the necessary qualifications.

Beresford wrote a large body of work across many genres and is now noted for his early science fiction work as well as his horror and ghost short stories.

John Davys Beresford died on 2nd February 1947 at the age of 73.

TO WALTER DE LA MARE

"Hath serving nature, bidden of the gods,
Thick-screened Man's narrow sky,
And hung these Stygian veils of fog
To hide his dingied sty?—
The gods who yet, at mortal birth,
Bequeathed him fantasy?"

'FOG' by WALTER DE LA MARE

Index of Contents

PROLOGUE

THE APPEARANCE OF MAN: A PLAY OUT OF TIME & SPACE

When the curtain rises, two men and a woman are discovered talking before an illimitable background.

FIRST MAN [Shaking hands with the man and the woman]
Well! Who'd have thought of meeting you here!

WOMAN
Or you, as far as that goes. We thought you were living in Putney.

FIRST MAN
So I am. It just happened that I'd run over this morning.

[Enter R. a nebula, spinning slowly. It passes majestically across the background as the scene proceeds.

SECOND MAN
The world's a very small place.

FIRST MAN
Ah! You're right, it is.

WOMAN
And how's the family?

FIRST MAN
Capital, thanks. Yours well, too, I hope?

WOMAN
All except Johnnie.

[Enter R. a group of prehistoric animals; a few brontosauri, titanotheres, mammoths, sabre-toothed tigers, and so on.

SPIRIT OF FIRST MAN
Well, I suppose I ought to be getting along.

SPIRIT OF SECOND MAN
Glad to have met you, anyway.

SPIRIT OF WOMAN
Funny our running up against you like this. As you said, the world's a very small place. Remember me to the family.

[They go out.

[The nebula, still spinning slowly, passes of the stage L.

CURTAIN AD LIB.

SIGNS & WONDERS

I dreamed this in the dullness of a February day in London.

I had been pondering the elements that go to the making of the human entity, and more particularly that new aspect of the theory of the etheric body which presents it as a visible, ponderable, tangible, highly organised, but almost incredibly tenuous, form of matter. From that I slid to the consideration of the possibility of some essence still more remote from our conception of the gross material of our objective experience; and then for a moment I held the idea of the imperceptible transition from this ultimately dispersing matter to thought or impulse—from the various bodies, etheric, astral, mental, causal, or Buddhistic, to the free and absolute Soul.

I suppose that at this point I fell asleep. I was not aware of any change of consciousness, but I cannot otherwise explain the fact that in an instant I was transported from an open place in the North of London, and from all this familiar earth of ours, to some planet without the knowledge of the dwellers in the solar system.

This amazing change was accomplished without the least shock. It was, indeed, imperceptible. The new world upon which I opened my eyes appeared at first sight to differ in no particular from that I had so recently left. I saw below me a perfect replica of the Hampstead Garden Suburb. The wind blew from the east with no loss of its characteristic quality. The occasional people who passed had the same air of tired foreboding and intense preoccupation with the miserable importance of their instant lives, that has seemed to me to mark the air of the middle-classes for the past few weeks. Also it was, I thought, beginning to rain.

I shivered and decided that I might as well go home. I felt that it was not worth while to travel a distance unrecordable in any measure of earthly miles, only to renew my terrestrial experiences. And then, by an accident, possibly to verify my theory that it was certainly going to rain, I looked up and realised at once the unspeakable difference between that world and our own.

For on this little earth of ours the sky makes no claim on our attention. It has its effects of cloud and light occasionally, and these effects no doubt may engage at times the interest of the poet or the artist. But to us, ordinary people, the sky is always pretty much the same, and we only look at it when we are expecting rain. Even then we often shut our eyes.

In that other world which revolves round a sun so distant that the light of it has not yet reached the earth the sky is quite different. Things happen in it. As I looked up, for instance, I saw a great door open, and out of it there marched an immense procession that trailed its glorious length across the whole width of heaven. I heard no sound. The eternal host moved in silent dignity from zenith to horizon. And after the procession had passed the whole visible arch of the sky was parted like a curtain and there looked out from the opening the semblance of a vast, intent eye.

But what immediately followed the gaze of that overwhelming watcher I do not know, for someone touched my arm, and a voice close at my shoulder said in the very tones of an earthly cockney:

"What yer starin' at, guv'nor? Airyplanes? I can't see none."

I looked at him and found that he was just such a loafer as one may see any day in London.

"Aeroplanes," I repeated. "Great Heaven, can't you see what's up there? The procession and that eye?"

He stared up then, and I with him, and the eye had gone; but between the still parted heavens I could see into the profundity of a space so rich with beauty and, as it seemed, with promise, that I held my breath in sheer wonder.

"No! I can't see nothin', guv'nor," my companion said.

And I presume that as he spoke I must have waked from my dream, for the glory vanished and I found myself dispensing a small alms to a shabby man who was representing himself as most unworthily suffering through no fault of his own.

As I walked home through the rain I reflected that the people of that incredibly distant world, walking, as they always do, with their gaze bent upon the ground, are probably unable to see the signs and wonders that blaze across the sky. They, like ourselves, are so preoccupied with the miserable importance of their instant lives.

THE CAGE

I was not asleep. I have watched passengers who kept their eyes shut between the stations, but as yet I have not seen an indisputable case of anyone sound asleep on the Hampstead and Charing Cross Tube. Of the other passages that make up London's greater intestine I have less experience, and it may be that some tubes are more conducive to slumber than the one most familiar to me. I have no ambition to make a dogmatic generalisation concerning either the stimulative or soporific action of the Underground. I merely wish it to be understood that I was not asleep, and that it was hardly possible that I could have been, with a small portmanteau permanently on one foot, and the owner of it—a little man who must have wished that the straps were rather longer—intermittently on the other. Against this, however, I have to put the fact that I could not say at which station the little man removed from me the burden of himself and his portmanteau. Nor could I give particulars of the appearance of such of my innumerable fellow-passengers as were most nearly presented to me, although I do know that most of them were reading—even the strap-hangers. It was, indeed, this observation that started my vision or train of thought or preoccupation—call it anything you like except a dream.

The eyes in his otherwise repulsive face held a wistfulness, a hint of vague speculation that attracted me. He sat, hunched on the summit of the steeply rising ground overlooking the sea, the place where the forest comes so abruptly to an end that from a little distance it looks as if it had been gigantically planed to a hard edge.

He was alone and ruminatively quiescent after food. He had fed well and carelessly. Some of the bones that lay near him had been very indifferently picked. He leaned forward clasping his hairy legs with his equally hairy arms, and stared out with that hint of speculation and wistfulness in his eyes over the placid magnificence of the Western Sea—just disturbed enough to reflect a gorgeous road of fire that laid a vanishing track across the waters up to the open goal of the low sun. A faint breeze blew up the hill, and it seemed as if he leant his face forward to drink the first refreshment of that sweet, cool air.

I approached him more nearly, trying to read his thought, rejoicing in the knowledge that he could neither see nor apprehend me. For though a man may know something of the past, the future is hidden from him, and I represented to him a future that could only be reckoned in a vast procession of centuries. Yet as I came nearer, so near that I could rest my hands on his knees and gaze up closely into his eyes, he shrank a little and leaned slightly away from me, as if he were uncertainly aware of an unfamiliar, distasteful presence. I fancied that the mat of hair on his chest just perceptibly bristled.

I could read his thought, now, and I was thrilled to discover that the expression of his eyes had not misled me. He had attained to a form of consciousness. He, alone, of all the beasts had received the gift of constructive imagination. He could look forward, make plans to meet a possible emergency. He knew already something of tomorrow. Even then he was deep in speculation. That day he had hunted a slow but cunning little beast which found a refuge among the great boulders that lay piled in gigantic profusion along the foreshore. And he had failed. Another quarry had been his, but that particular little beast had outwitted him. And now, longing for it, he ruminated clumsy lethargic plans for its capture.

It may have been that the unusual effort tired him, for presently he slept, still hunched into the same compact heap, crouching with an effect of swift alertness as if he were ready at the least alarm to leap up and vanish into the cover of the forest.

Then, a plan came to me, also. I would bring a vision to this primitive ancestor of mankind. I would merge myself with his being and he should dream a dream of the immensely distant future. Blessed and privileged above all the human race, he should know for an instant to what inconceivable developments, to what towering heights of intellectual and manipulative glory his descendants should one day be heir. I had no definite idea of the precise illustration I should choose to set forth the magnificence of man's latest attainment. Nor did I pause to consider what I myself might suffer in the process of this infamous liaison between the ages. I acted on an impulse that I found irresistible. I have myself longed so often to read the distant future of mankind, that I felt as a god bestowing an inestimable gift. But I should have known that in the mystical union it is the god and not the man who suffers.

I was wrapped in an awful darkness as we fell stupendously through time, but presently I knew that we were rising again, weighted with the burden of primitive flesh. Then in an instant came a strange yellow unnatural light, the roaring of a terrible sound—and the fearful vision. The horror of it was unendurable; the shock of it so great that spirit and flesh were rent asunder. I remained. He fell back to the sweetness of the cool air blowing up from the tranquil sea.

Did he rush frantically into the forest or sit with dripping mouth and wide alarmed eyes, rigidly staring at the scarlet rim of the setting sun? Yet what could he have understood of the future in that moment of detestable revelation? Could he have recognised men and women in their strange disguise of modern dress, as being even of the same species as himself? And if he had, what could he have known of them, seeing them packed so closely together, immoveably wedged into the terror of that rocking roaring cage of unknown material; seeing them occupied in staring so intently and incomprehensibly at those amazing little black-dotted white sheets? Impossible for him to guess that those speckled sheets held a magic that transported his descendants from the misery of their cage into imaginations so extensive and so various that some of them might, however dimly and allusively, include himself, hunched and ruminant, regarding the vast tranquillity of the sea.

The tunnel suddenly broke, the roaring gave place to a rattle that by contrast was gentle and soothing. I opened my eyes. We were under the sky again, slipping, with intermittent flashes of light, into the harbour of Golder's Green Station.

For a moment, I seemed to see the clumsy and violent shape of a beast that strove in panic to escape; and then I came back to my own world of the patient readers, with their white, controlled faces, forming now in solemn procession down the aisle of the carriage.

But it was his dream, not mine. And I have been wondering whether, if I dreamed also, the distant future might not seem equally unendurable to me?

ENLARGEMENT

When he heard the first signal, warning the people of London to take cover, his spirit revolted.

He began to picture with a sick disgust the scene of his coming confinement in the dirty basement. Mrs. Gibson, his landlady, would welcome him with the air of forced cheerfulness he knew so well. She would make the same remarks about the noise of the guns. She would say again: "Well, there's one thing, it drowns the noise of the bombs—if they've really got here this time." Then Maunders from the first floor would say that you could always pick out the sound of the aerial torpedoes; and explain, elaborately, why. Mrs. Graham from the second floor would say that she'd rather enjoy it, if it weren't for the children. And her eldest little prig of a boy would say, "I'm not afraid, mumma," and expect everyone to praise his courage. Mrs. Gibson would praise him, of course. She would say: "There, now, I declare he's the bravest of anyone." She was obliged to do it. She would never be able to get new lodgers this winter. And when that preliminary talk was done with, they would all begin again on the endlessly tedious topic of reprisals; and keep it up until a pause in the barrage set them on to spasmodic ejaculations of wonder whether "they" had been driven off, or gone, or been shot down, or....

No; definitely, he would not stand it. He could better endure the simultaneous explosion of every gun in London than three hours of that conversation. Moreover, he could not face the horrible drip, drip, from the scullery sink. On the night of the last raid he had been very near the sink. And the thought of that steady plop ... plop ... of water into the galley-pot Mrs. Gibson kept under the tap for some idiotic reason, was as the thought of an inferno such as could not have been conceived by Dante, nor organised by the Higher German Command.

Nerves? He shrugged his shoulders. In a sense, no doubt. Suspense, dread, a long exasperation of waiting had filled every commonplace experience—more particularly that dreadful dripping of the cold water tap—with all kinds of horrible associations. But if it was "nerves," it was not nervousness, not fear of being killed, nothing in the least like panic. He was quite willing to face the possible danger of the open streets. But he could not and would not face Mrs. Gibson and the scullery sink.

No; he must escape—a fugitive from protection. Men had fled from strange things, but had they ever fled from a stranger thing than refuge? He must go secretly. If Mrs. Gibson heard him she would stop him, begin an immense, unendurable argument. She could not afford to risk the loss of a lodger this winter. She would bring Maunders and Mrs. Graham to join her in persuasion and protest. Freedom was hard to win in London, in such times as these.

He crept down the long three flights of stairs like some wary criminal feeling his cautious way to liberty. But once he had, with infinite deliberation, slipped back the ailing latch of the front door, he lifted his head and squared his shoulders with a great gasp of relief. He could have wept tears of exultation. He was filled with a deep thankfulness for this boon of his enlargement....

There was no sound of guns as yet; nor any sweep of searchlights tormenting the wide gloom of the sky. It was a wonderful, calm night; a little misty on the ground; but, above, the moon was serene and bright as a new guinea.

He had no hesitation as to his direction. He desired the greatest possible expansion of outlook; and turned his face at once towards the river. On the Embankment he would be able to see a wide arc of the sky. He had a sense of setting about a prohibited adventure, full of the most daring and delicious excitements. His one dread was that he might be interfered with, stopped, sent home.

The cycling policemen looked at him, he thought, with peculiar suspicion. They gruffly shouted at him to take cover, with a curt note of warning, as if he were breaking the law by indulging himself in this escapade. He tried to avoid notice by slinking into the shadows. That cold, inimical moonlight made everything so conspicuous....

Except for the policemen, the streets were vividly empty. He could feel the spirit of London crouched in expectancy. Behind every darkened window men, women, and children waited and longed for the relief of the first gun. And while they waited they chattered and smiled. And all their laughter and conversation was like these streets, vividly empty; their spirits had taken cover.

He alone was free, exempt, rejoicing in his liberty....

The ground mist was thicker on the Embankment; and for a moment he was confused by the loom of a strange obelisk that had a curiously remote, exotic air in the midst of this familiar London. Then he recognised the outline as that of Cleopatra's Needle, and went close up to the alien monument of another age and stared up at it in the proclamatory moonlight. He wondered if any magic lingered in those cryptic inscriptions? If they might not have endowed the very granite with curious, occult powers. He was still staring at the solemn portent of the obelisk when the barrage opened with unusual suddenness....

For a time he was crushed and overwhelmed by the pressure of that intimidating fury of sound. He cowered and winced like a naked soul exposed to the intimate vengeance of God. He was as beaten and battered by the personal threat of those cumulative explosions as if every gun sought him and him alone as the objective of its awful wrath.

But, by degrees, he began to grow accustomed even to that world-rocking pandemonium. He became aware of the undertones that laced the dominant roar and thunder of artillery. He could trace, he believed, beside the shriek of shell, the humming whirr of an aeroplane he could not see. And once something whizzed past him with a high singing hiss that ended abruptly with a sharp clip. He guessed that a fragment of shrapnel had buried itself in one of the plane-trees.

Yet the real danger of that warning did not terrify him as had the enormous onslaught of noise from the barrage. At the next intermission of the deafening bombardment he stood up, rested his hand on the plinth of the obelisk, and stared, wondering and unafraid, into the great arc of the sky. He could see no aeroplanes.... The stillness was so profound that he could hear with a grateful distinctness the soft clucking ripple of the rising flood.

Presently he dropped his regard for the heavens to the plain objective of deserted London. The mist had almost dispersed in some places, had thickened in others—churned and driven, perhaps, by the vast pressure of the sound waves. Across the road he could see the impending cliff of great buildings, pale and tall in the moonlight. At his feet the plane-trees threw trembling, skeleton shadows. All the town waited in suspense to know whether or not the bombardment would presently be renewed.

He had a presentiment that it was all over. He felt the quick exaltation and vigour of one who has suffered and escaped danger. But when he looked up the Embankment and saw what he took to be the silhouettes of three towering trams emerging with furtive silence from the mist, he was aware of a faint sense of disappointment. Nothing was left to him but to return to the common dreariness of life.

He took a step towards the trams that were advancing with such a stately, such a hushed and ponderous deliberation....

Trams...?

He held his breath, staring and gaping, and then backed nervously against the pedestal of the great Egyptian monument.

Had the shock of that awful bombardment broken his nerve? Was he mad? Bewitched by some ancient magic? Or was it, perhaps, that in one swift inappreciable moment he had been instantly killed by a fragment of shrapnel, and that, now, his emerging spirit could, even as it watched these familiar surroundings, peer back deep into the hidden mysteries of time?

He pressed himself, shivering and fascinated, against the hard, insistent reality of cold granite; but still in single file these three colossal shapes advanced, solemn and majestic, rocking magnificently with a slow and powerful gravity.

They were almost abreast of him now, sombre and stolid—three vast, prehistoric, unattended Elephants, imperturbably exploring the silences of this dead and lonely city.

They passed, and left him weak and trembling, but indescribably happy.

Two minutes later, a blind and insensible policeman, following the very path of those magical evocations of the thought of ancient Egypt, rode carelessly by, bearing the banal message that all was clear.

But the adventurer walked home in a dream of ecstasy. Whatever the future might hold for him, he had pierced the veil of the commonplace. He had seen and heard on the Thames Embankment that sacred, mystical procession of the Elephants.

He looked at Mrs. Gibson with something of contempt when she brought him his breakfast next morning. He could not respond to her chatter concerning the foolish detail of last night's raid. She, poor woman, was afraid that she might, in some unknown way, have offended him. Her last effort was meant as an amiable diversion. One never knew whether people weren't more scared than they chose to admit.

"There's one amusin' bit," she said, laying his morning paper on the table, "as I just glanced at while I was waitin' for the water to boil. It's in Hincidents of the Raid. It seems as three performin' elephunts goin' 'ome from the 'Ippodrome or somewhere got loose—their keeper done a bolt, I suppose, when the guns began—and got walkin' off by theirselves all down the Embankment. They must 'a been a comic sight, poor things. Terrified they was, no doubt...."

Now, why should God explain his miracles through the mouth of a Mrs. Gibson?

THE PERFECT SMILE

The realisation of it first came to Douglas Owen when he was not quite five years old.

From his babyhood he had been spoilt, more particularly by his father. He could be such a charming little boy, and his frequent outbreaks of real naughtiness were overlooked or gently reproved. They were even admired in private by his parents, who regarded these first signs of disobedience, temper, and selfishness as the marks of an independent and original spirit.

Nevertheless, when Douglas was nearly five years old, he achieved a minor climax that the most indulgent father could not overlook. Despite all warnings and commands, Douglas would steal from the larder. When there were cakes or tarts he took those for preference, but when there was nothing else he would steal bread, merely, as it seemed, for the pleasure of stealing it. His father had protested to his mother that everything should be kept under lock and key, but as Mrs. Owen explained: "You can't expect a cook to be for ever locking things up." And the little Douglas was ingenious in his depredations.

He chose his moment with cunning. Also he knew, as the cook herself confessed, how "to get round her."

Mr. Owen, who was a tender-hearted idealist, admitted at last that stern measures were called for, and he took Douglas into his study and remonstrated with him gently, even lovingly, but with great earnestness. The remonstrance gained strength from Mrs. Owen's fear that Douglas might make himself seriously ill by his illicit feastings. Douglas, who was forward for his age, listened with attention to his father's serious lecture and promised reform. "I won't do it again, father. Promise," he said with apparent sincerity. And his father, believing absolutely in his child's truthfulness, and remembering his wife's adjuration to be "really firm," was tempted to clinch the thing once for all by issuing an ultimatum.

"I'm sure you won't, little son," he said, "because you see if you did, daddy would have to whack you. He'd hate doing it, but he'd have to do it all the same."

Douglas's expression was faintly speculative. He had heard something like this before, from his mother.

"But you've promised faithfully that you'll never, never take anything out of the larder, or the kitchen, or the pantry again, haven't you, darling?" Mr. Owen persisted, by way of having everything quite clear.

"Promised faithfully," agreed Douglas; parted from his father with a hug of forgiveness; and was found a quarter of an hour later in the larder, eating jam with a spoon from a newly-opened jar.

"You threatened to whack him if he didn't keep his promise, and you must do it," Mrs. Owen said firmly to her husband. "If you don't keep your promises, how can you expect him to keep his?"

"Damn!" murmured Mr. Owen with great intensity.

"I shall bring him in and leave him with you," his wife said, correctly interpreting her husband's method of reluctantly accepting the inevitable.

Douglas was brought, and it was evident that on this occasion he was truly conscious of sin and apprehensive of the result. All his nonchalance was gone from him. He did not cry, but his eyes were wide and terrified. He looked a thoroughly guilty and scared child.

Mr. Owen hardened his heart. He thought of the contempt shown for his authority, of the wilfully broken promise, and of the threat to his son's future unless he were made to realise that sin cannot go unpunished.

Mrs. Owen, looking at her husband's stern face, was satisfied that justice would be done.

And then, when father and son were alone and sentence had been pronounced, the smile came for the first time.

Douglas did not know why or how it came. He was only conscious of it as something that illuminated his whole being, put him among the angels, and gave him immunity from all earthly terrors.

To his father, the smile was simply blinding. It was so radiant, so tender, forgiving, and altogether godlike. It condescended to his weakness and mortality, and made him feel how unworthy he was of such splendid recognition. His little son's face glowed with a perfect consciousness of power, and yet he seemed to surrender himself with a dignified humility to this threatened infamy of corporal punishment. Moreover, it was a smile that expressed the ultimate degree of innocence. It was impossible for anyone who saw it to believe that Douglas could have sinned in perversity, or with any evil intention.

And there was one other amazing peculiarity about this rare smile of Douglas's, for it not only permeated the finer feelings of those who witnessed it, but was also reflected weakly in their faces, as the outer and larger rainbow reflects the intensified beauty of the inner.

So now Mr. Owen's smile faintly echoed his son's.

"I'm sorry, Daddy," said Douglas confidently.

And Mrs. Owen waiting outside, listening in tremulous agitation for the wail that should announce her husband's resolution, heard no sound. And presently Douglas came out, still wearing the last pale evidences of his recent halo.

"But why didn't you?" Mrs. Owen asked her husband, when their son was out of earshot. She would have overlooked the essential omission, almost with gratitude, if she had not believed it her duty to reprove her husband's characteristic weakness.

"He—he smiled," Mr. Owen said.

"But Harold!" his wife protested.

Mr. Owen wrinkled his forehead and looked exceedingly distressed. "I don't know that I can explain," he said. "It wasn't an ordinary smile. I've never seen him do it before. I—I have never seen anything like it. I can only say that I would defy anyone to punish him when he smiled like that."

"I noticed as he came out...." began Mrs. Owen.

"It was practically over then," her husband interrupted, and added with a slightly literary turn of speech he sometimes adopted: "That was only the afterglow."

But it is worth recording that, from that time, Douglas, although he was naughty enough in other ways, never robbed the larder again.

Nine years passed before Douglas's great gift was once more manifested.

There was undoubtedly something unusually charming about the boy that protected him from punishment; and as he had been spoilt by his father at home, so was he also treated rather too leniently at school. But Dr. Watson, his headmaster, came at last to the end of his weakness. Douglas was becoming a bad influence in the school. His careless evasions of discipline set an example of insubordination that was all too readily followed by the other boys.

Dr. Watson braced himself to the inevitable. In his heart he regretted the necessity, but he knew that Douglas must be sacrificed for the good of the school. He had been warned and mildly punished a hundred times. Now he must pay the full penalty.

The choice lay between expulsion and a public flogging, and when Douglas chose the latter, Dr. Watson resolved that the flogging should be of unusual severity. When the whole school was assembled, he made a very earnest and moving speech, deploring the causes that had given rise to the occasion, and showing how inevitable was the disgraceful result.

Douglas, white and terrified, made ready in a trembling silence, then, turning his back on the tensely expectant audience, he faced his headmaster.

Arthur Coburn, Douglas's humanitarian house-master, was so upset by these preliminaries that for one moment he was tempted to leave the hall. Corporal punishment had always seemed to him a horrible thing, but never had it seemed quite so revolting as on this occasion. Yet he fought against the feeling. He knew that his chief was neither a stern nor a cruel man, and had been driven into the present position by the sheerly impudent persistence of Douglas's disobedience. By way of alleviating as far as possible his own nervous distress, therefore, Coburn took up a position with his back to the rostrum, and faced the great crowd of just perceptibly intimidated boys.

And waiting, much as Douglas's mother had waited in shamed anxiety some nine years before, Coburn was amazed to see a sudden and incomprehensible change in the massed faces before him. The tensity, the look of half eager, half apprehensive expectation strangely relaxed. A wave of what looked like relief ran back in a long ripple of emotion from the front to the back of the many ranks of watching boys. In one instant everyone was wearing a faint smile of almost holy serenity.

Coburn turned with a leap of astonishment and stared at Dr. Watson. And the smile he saw on the headmaster's face outshone that on the faces of his audience as the sun outshines the moon.

But no one save Dr. Watson saw the perfect radiance that flowed out from the face of Douglas Owen....

"I'm sorry, sir," was all that Douglas said.

Dr. Watson dropped his birch as if it had burnt him.

His second address to the school was hesitating and apologetic. He tried to explain that when the clear signs of repentance and of reform were so evident as they were in the case of Owen, corporal punishment was superfluous and would be little short of criminal. Yet even Coburn, who so profoundly agreed with the principle expounded, found the explanation unsatisfying. He could not help feeling that Dr. Watson was concealing his true reason.

Nevertheless, it is well to note that after this reprieve Douglas passed the remainder of his school-life without committing any other serious offence.

He was only thirty-two when he came before the last and most terrible tribunal possible in our society.

After he left Cambridge, he was taken into a city office by a friend of his father's. Everyone liked him, and he might have made an excellent position for himself if he had not led such a loose life out of business hours. He seemed unable to resist any temptation, and the inevitable result was that he got into debt.

When his father's friend discovered the extent of Douglas's thefts from the firm, he had no choice but to dismiss him; although for the young man's sake not less than for the sake of his friendship with his father, he never even threatened prosecution.

For a time Douglas lived at home. Later he went to Canada for a couple of years. Then his father died, leaving him some five or six thousand pounds, and he came home again—to spend it. When that money was all gone, he lived on the charity of his many friends. They all knew him for an incorrigible scamp, but he still retained much of his old charm.

The crime for which he came at last to be tried for his life at the Old Bailey was too disgraceful an affair to be reported in detail. The only possible defence was that Douglas was unquestionably drunk when the murder was actually committed. Yet despite the weakness of the case for the defending counsel, everyone in court including the jury and possibly even Lord Justice Ducie himself, could not restrain a feeling of sympathy for the prisoner. He had not lost, despite all his excesses, his engaging air of ingenuous youth. And his manner throughout the trial naturally evoked a strong sense of pity.

The jury did all they could for him by bringing in a verdict of manslaughter.

The judge leaned forward with a kindly, almost fatherly air, as he asked the prisoner if he had anything to say in his own defence.

And at that supreme moment, as he stood white and terrified in the dock, Douglas was aware that once more, for the third time in his life, that wonderful glow of power, peace, and condescension was beginning to thrill through him.

He straightened himself and raised his head. He looked the judge in the face. He believed that the perfect smile had come again to save him. But he looked in vain for the old response.

The judge's mouth had twitched as Douglas looked at him, and for one instant all those who were waiting so anxiously for the pronouncement of the sentence were astounded to see a look of horrible bestiality flicker across the face of the old man who was accounted the most gentle and philanthropic judge who had ever sat in the criminal court. It was only a momentary impression, for Lord Ducie at once put both hands before his face as if to shut off the sight of some terrible infamy; but Bateson, the defending counsel, who was watching the judge, says that he never afterwards could quite recover his old respect for him.

It is unquestionably true that the hideous, depraved, and insulting grimace which had so unexpectedly revealed the soul of Douglas Owen, was solely responsible for the maximum sentence of twenty years' penal servitude that was imposed upon him.

If a man continually flouts the angels of grace, he must expect at last to be delivered over to the devil he so devotedly serves.

THE HIDDEN BEAST

His house is the last in the village. Towards the forest the houses become more and more scattered, reaching out to the wild of the wood as if they yearned to separate themselves from the swarm that clusters about the church and the inn. And his house has taken so long a stride from the others that it is held to the village by no more than the slender thread of a long footpath. Yet the house is set with its face towards us, and has an air of resolutely holding on to the safety of our common life, as if dismayed at its boldness in swimming so far it had turned and desperately grasped the life-line of that footpath.

He lived alone, a strange man, surly and reticent. Some said that he had a sinister look; and on those rare occasions when he joined us at the inn, after sunset, he sat aside and spoke little.

I was surprised when, as we came out of the inn one night, he took my arm and asked me if I would go home with him. The moon was at the full, and the black shadows of the dispersing crowd that lunged down the street seemed to gesticulate an alarm of weird dismay. The village was momentarily mad with the clatter of footsteps and the noise of laughter, and somewhere down towards the forest a dog was baying.

I wondered if I had not misunderstood him.

As he watched my hesitation his face pleaded with me. "There are times when a man is glad of company," he said.

We spoke little as we passed through the village towards the silences of his lonely house. But when we came to the footpath he stopped and looked back.

"I live between two worlds," he said, "the wild and ..."—he paused before he rejected the obvious antithesis, and concluded—"the restrained."

"Are we so restrained?" I asked, staring at the huddle of black-and-silver houses clinging to their refuge on the hill.

He murmured something about a "compact," and my thoughts turned to the symbol of the chalk-white church-tower that dominated the honeycomb of the village.

"The compact of public opinion," he said more boldly.

My imagination lagged. I was thinking less of him than of the transfiguration of the familiar scene before me. I did not remember ever to have studied it thus under the reflections of a full moon. An echo of his word, differently accented, drifted through my mind. I saw our life as being in truth compact, little and limited.

He took up his theme again when we had entered the house and were facing each other across the table, in a room that looked out over the forest. The shutters were unfastened, the window open, and I could see how, on the further shore of the waste-lands, the light feebly ebbed and died against the black cliff of the wood.

"We have to choose between freedom and safety," he said. "The individual is too wild and dangerous for the common life. He must make his agreement with the community; submit to become a member of the people's body. But I"—he paused and laughed—"I have taken the liberty of looking out of the back window."

While he spoke I had been aware of a sound that seemed to come from below the floor of the room in which we were sitting. And when he laughed I fancied that I heard the response of a snuffling cry.

He looked at me mockingly across the table.

"It's an echo from the jungle," he said. "Some trick of reflected sound. I can always hear it in this room at night."

I shivered and stood up. "I prefer the safety of our common life," I told him. "It may be that I have a limited mind and am afraid, but I find my happiness in the joys of security and shelter. The wild terrifies me."

"A limited mind?" he commented. "Probably it is rather that you lack a fire in the blood."

I was glad to leave him, and he on his part made no effort to detain me.

It was not long after this visit of mine that the people first began to whisper about him in the village. At the beginning they brought no charge against him, talking only of his strangeness and of his separation from our common interests. But presently I heard a story of some fierce wild animal that he caged and tortured in the prison of his house. One said that he had heard it screaming in the night, and another that he had heard it beating against the door. And some argued that it was a threat to our safety, since the beast might escape and make its way into the village; and some that such brutality, even though it were to a wild animal, could not be tolerated. But I wondered inwardly whether the affair were any business of ours so long as he kept the beast to himself.

I was a member of the Council that year, and so took part in the voting when presently the case was laid before us. But no vote of mine would have helped him if I had dared to overcome my reluctance and speak in his favour. For whatever reservations may have been secretly withheld by the members of the Council, they were unanimous in condemning him.

We went, six of us, in full daylight, to search his house. He received us with a laugh, and told us that we might seek at our leisure. But though we sought high and low, peering and tapping, we found no evidence that any wild thing had ever been concealed there.

And within a month of the day of our search he left the village.

I saw him alone once before he went, and he told me that he had chosen for the wild and freedom, that he could no longer endure to be held to the village even by the thread of the footpath.

But he did not thank me for having allowed the search of his house to be conducted by daylight, although he knew that I at least was sure no echo of the forest could be heard in that little room of his save in the transfigured hours between the dusk and the dawn.

A STUDY IN EXTROVERSION

My friend has a wonderful voice, a primitive voice, open-throated and resonant, the great chest roar of the wild. When he shouts he does it without visible effort. The full red of his face may deepen to the opening shades of purple, but that evidence of constriction is due solely to emotion. The lift of a major third in his tone is accomplished without any appearance of muscular effort. He opens another cylinder and lets the additional power find its own pitch in the reverberating brass of the fog-horn. And the effect is as if the devastating crash of the barrage had come suddenly and horribly near. Perhaps, for one instant, the attack of his voice ceases, and then while the room still trembles to the echo of his last statement, the barrage leaps forward and spills its explosion into the secret refuges of my being.

Behind that cover, the sense of the statements he gives forth with such enormous assurance creeps up and falls upon me while I am still insensible. It is as though his argument bayoneted me treacherously while I am paralysed from shock. If my mind were free I could defeat the simple attack of his argument; but should I be given one trifling opportunity for speech I can never take it. My mind is battered, crushed and inert. I dare not lift my head for fear of exposing myself again to that awful approach of the barrage.

My friend has described himself so conclusively in a term of the old free-trade dispute, that nothing could be added to enlighten his definition. He is, and prides himself vociferously on the fact, a whole-hogger. He gets that off on his lower register which is just bearable. There is no need for the barrage to defend the approach of that statement. It is self-evident. The great welt of his boots, massive as an Egyptian plinth; the stiff hairiness of his bristling tweeds; the honest amazement of his ripe face; the very solidity of the signet ring that is nevertheless not too heavy for his hirsute finger—all these proclaim him as the type and consummation of the whole-hogger.

He adopted the label with pride some time in the middle 'nineties, when he was already a mature, determined and unalterable man of twenty-eight. He was a fervent patriot throughout the Boer War. He has, since December, 1905, spent a fount of energy that would have wrecked the physique of ten average men in denouncing such things as Education Bills, Old Age Pensions, the Reform of the House of Lords, Home Rule—in brief, the Government—or, as he always called it, "this Government." And since the beginning of the war he has demonstrated—proving every statement of the Times by the evidence of the Daily Mail—that there will never be any truth or sanity in the world until the whole German race is beaten to its perjured knees (his metaphors sometimes have an effect of concentration); until it is so thrashed, scourged, humiliated, broken and defeated (a barrage is necessarily redundant) that the last remaining descendants of the Prussian shall crawl, pitifully exposed and humbled, about the earth, begging God and man for forgiveness.

My friend is, in fact, the perfect type of what is known to psycho-analysts as the extrovert. He has never questioned himself, never doubted the infallibility of his own gospel, never known fear. He does not understand the meaning of the word introspection, and feels nothing but pity for a man who halts between two opinions. He divides all mankind into two categories—splendid fellows and damned fools—although I have found the suggestion of a third division in his description of a querulous Tory as "a damned fool on the right side." On the wrong side, however, there are no splendid fellows. As he says, he "hasn't patience" with anyone who is either so thick-headed or so unscrupulous as to disagree with him in politics.

By way of a hobby he farms 800 acres of land, and he has never had any trouble with his labourers. I will admit that he is generous with a careless, exuberant generosity that does not ask for gratitude. But it is not his generosity that has won for him the devotion of his servants and employees. They bow before his certainty. He is a religion to them, a trustworthy holdfast in this world of unstable things.

And I suppose that is also why he is still "my friend." His conversation is nothing but a string of affirmations with none of which I can agree. He is an intolerable bore, and his voice hurts me. But I regard him with wonder and admiration, and when the terrors and oppressions of the world threaten to break my spirit I go to him for strength.

In the early days of our acquaintanceship I used to try, by facial contortions and parenthetic gesture, to indicate my paltry disagreement with his political and social creed. Perhaps I came near at that time to inclusion in the "Damfool" category; but the nearness of my house, his generosity in overlooking the preliminary marks of my idiocy, and (deciding factor) the inappeasable craving for company which is his only means of expression, influenced him to give me another and yet another chance. He took to putting up the barrage at the least sign of my disapproval, and so converted me—outwardly. While I am with him I relax myself. I stare at him and wonder. I sometimes find myself wishing that I could be like him!

It was, indeed, the thought of so impossible and outrageous an ambition that prompted me to attempt this portrait of him. I have failed, I know, to convey his proper quality. Anyone who has never met my friend will find nothing but the echo and shadow of him in this sketch. But is there anyone who has not met him or some member of his family? Down here I associate him with the land, but he has business interests connected with the Stock Exchange. And he has brothers, uncles and sons—any number of them—all of the same virtue. They are in the Army, the Law, Medicine, in the Pulpit, in Trade, in the House—in everything. They are all successful, and they have all given their services with immense vigour and volubility to the great task that my friend defines as "downing the Hun." They are all men of action, and their thinking is done by a method as simple as simple addition. A few sterling principles are taken for granted, principles that can be applied in such phrases as "the good of the country," "playing the game," "Rome was not built in a day," or "what I go by is facts," and from these elementary premises any and every argument can be deduced by the two-plus-two method. It is the apotheosis and triumph of a priorism. They do not believe in induction, and what they do not believe in does not exist for them. Their strength is in loudness and confidence, and they are very strong.

Nevertheless, puzzling over my friend and his family in my own hair-splitting way, I have been wondering if this loudness is not a sign that the family has lost something of its old power? Their ancestors, also, were men of simple ideas and strong passions, men of inflexible purpose. But they were not, so far as one can judge from history, so blatantly loud. They bear the same kind of relation to my friend that Lincoln does to Roosevelt.

Is the type changing, I ask myself, or only the conditions? And if the latter, is the man of intense convictions and rigid principles become so much of an anomaly in this new world of ours that the development of the barrage has become necessary as a means of assertion against a people who will question even such a simple premiss as that two added to two invariably produces four? For they do that. Your characteristic man of the age will warn you that the mathematical statement is an assumption only, not a universal truth. He will probably add that in any case it is useless as an analogy, since it disregards entirely the qualitative value of "two."

From the over-conscientious mind such criticisms as this tear away the last hopes of stability. One loses faith in the Cosmos. But my friend smiles his pity for all such damfoolishness. His solid feet are planted on the solid earth. He knows that two and two make four. His ancestors have proved it by their actions. And if such silly questioning of sound principles is persisted in, he waves it aside and asserts himself in his usual effective way.

Nevertheless, as I have said, it seems that that form of barrage was once unnecessary.

THE INTROVERT

Nothing is more dispiriting than the practice of classifying humanity according to "types." Your professional psychologist does it for his own purposes. This is his way of collating material for the large generalisation he is always chasing. His ideal is a complete record. He would like to present us as so many samples on a labelled card—the differences between the samples on any one card being ascribed to an initial carelessness in manufacture. His method is the apotheosis of that of the gay Italian fortune-teller one used to see about the streets, with her little cage of love-birds that sized you up and picked you out a suitable future. Presently, we hope, the psychologist will be able to do that for us with a greater discrimination. He will take a few measurements, test our reaction times, consult an index, and hand us out an infallible analysis of our "type." After that we shall know precisely what we are fitted for, and whether our ultimate destination is the Woolsack or the Workhouse.

But your psychologist has his uses, and it is the amateur in this sort, particularly the novel-writing amateur, who arouses our protest. He—I use the pronoun asexually—does not spend himself in prophecy, but he deals us out into packs with an air of knowing just where we belong. And his novels prove how right he was, because you can prove anything in a novel. His readers like this method. It is easy to understand, and it provides them with an articulate description of the inevitable Jones.

I cling to that as some justification for the habit, as an excuse for my own exhibition of the weakness, however dispiriting. It is so convenient to have a shorthand reference for Jones and other of our acquaintances. The proper understanding of any one of them might engage the leisure of a lifetime; and if for general purposes we can tuck our friends into some neat category, we serve the purposes of lucidity.

Lastly, to conclude this apology, I would plead that a new scheme of classification, such as that provided by psycho-analysis, is altogether too fascinating to be resisted.

There is, for example, my friend David Wince, the typical "introvert," and an almost perfect foil for my friend the "extrovert," previously described. The two men loathe the sight of one another. Contempt on one side and fear on the other is a sufficient explanation of their mutual aversion. Wince, indeed, has an instinctive fear of anything that bellows, and a rooted distrust of most other things. He suffers from a kind of spiritual agoraphobia that makes him scared and suspicious of large generalisations, broad horizons and cognate phenomena. He likes, as he says, to be "sure of one step" before he takes the next. The open distances of a political argument astound and terrify him. He takes all discussions with a great seriousness, and displays an obstructive passion for definition and the right use of words. "What I should like to understand" is a favourite opening of his, and the thing he would like to understand is almost invariably some abstruse and fundamental definition.

The á priori method is anathema to him. He is, in fact, characteristically unable to comprehend it. He has little respect for a syllogism as such, because his mind seems to work backwards, and all his logical faculty is used in the dissection of premises. When my exasperation reaches the stage at which I say: "But, my dear fellow, let us take it for granted, for the sake of argument ..." he wrings his hands in despair and replies: "But that's the whole point. We can't take these things for granted. If you don't examine your premises, where are you?" He has a habit in conversation of emphasizing such words as those I have underlined, and a look of desolation comes into his face when he plaintively enquires where we are. At those times I see his timid, irresolute spirit momentarily staring aghast at the threat of this world's immense distances; before it ducks back with a sigh of relief into the shelter afforded by his introspective analyses. "Let us be quite sure of our ground," he says, "before we draw any deductions." His ground is, I fancy, a kind of "dug-out."

He has had an unfortunate matrimonial experience. His wife ran away with another man, some three or four years ago, and he is trying to screw himself up to the pitch of divorcing her. For a man of his sensitiveness, the giving of evidence in Court upon such a delicate subject will be a very trying ordeal. He has confided very little of his trouble to me, but occasional hints of his, and the reports of another friend who knew Mrs. Wince personally, lead me to suppose that she was rather a large-minded, robust sort of woman. Perhaps he bored her. I can imagine that he would bore anyone who had a lust for action; and as they had been married for eight years and had no children, I am not prepared to condemn Mrs. Wince, off-hand, for her desertion of him. I have no doubt that Wince might be able to make out a good ethical case for himself. I picture his attitude towards his wife as being extremely self-denying, deprecatory and almost passionately virtuous. But I prefer to reserve judgment on the issue between them. I can imagine that his habit of procrastinating may have annoyed her to desperation. He has told me with a kind of meek pride that he has often been to the door of a shop, and then postponed the purchase he had come to make until the next day. He loathes shopping. He finds the mildest shopkeeper an intimidating creature. I do not know what would happen to him if his hairdresser died. He has been to the same man for over twenty years.

In politics he is a conscientious Radical, and his one test of politicians is "Are they sincere?" He distrusts the Tories because he believes that they must be working for their own personal ends, but he has had a private weakness for Mr. Balfour ever since he read The Foundations of Belief. His hero is W. E. Gladstone, whose opinions represent to him, I fancy, some aspect of his own, while Gladstone's courage, Wince says, was "perfectly glorious."

He adores courage, but only when it is the self-conscious kind. Our friend Bellows, for instance, does not appear to Wince as brave, but as callous, thick-skinned, or "simply a braggart." All Wince's resentment comes to the surface when the two men meet by some untoward accident. On one such occasion he magnificently left the room and slammed the door after him, but I think that he probably regretted that act of violence before he reached home. He has a nervous horror of making enemies. He need have no fear in this case. Bellows considers Wince as beneath his notice, and always speaks of him to me as "your hair-splittin' friend."

Now that I have documented Wince I feel chiefly sorry for him, but when I am in his company I frequently have a strong desire to shake him. I wonder if his wife began by being sorry for him, and if her escapade was incidentally intended as a shaking? Did she flaunt her wickedness at him in the hope of "rousing him up"? If so, she failed, ignominiously. Shakings of that sort only aggravate his terror of life. Indeed, I do not think that anything can be done for him. If he survives the war, the coming of the New Democracy will certainly finish him. Talking of the possibility of a November Election, he told me that he meant to abstain from voting. He said that he could not vote for Lloyd George, and was afraid of putting too much power into the hands of the Labour Party. He did not think that they had yet had enough experience of government to be trusted with the control of a nation.

In the hallowed protections of the Victorian era he had his place and throve after his fashion. Life was so secure and the future apparently so certain. But he was not fitted to stand the strain of coming out into the open. He is horrified by the war, but in his heart he is still more horrified by the thought of the conditions that will come with peace. He sees the future, I know, as a vast, formless threat. He sees life exposed to a great gale of revolution. He is afraid that his retreat will be no longer available, that one day he will find his burrow stopped and himself called upon to face, and to work with, his fellow-men.

But no doubt his natural timidity tends to over-estimate the probability of these dangers.

THE BARRIER

The body seems to have a separate and industrious life of its own. It carries on works of amazing intricacy beyond the reach of consciousness; works, the very existence of which are unknown to us so long as they are being successfully performed. Only when there is some hitch or impediment, is the consciousness crudely signalled by the message of pain. Attention is demanded, but no detail is given of the nature of the trouble, nor of how it may be overcome. All that the message conveys is a plea for rest, for the suspension of those activities within the consciousness which are—may we assume?—using up energy from some additional source that the workers now wish to draw upon themselves.

Can we assume further, that this corporate life of the cells is not entirely mechanical; is not a series of chemico-biological reflexes or reactions, somehow mysteriously initiated at the birth of life and continued by the stimulus of some unknown unconscious force so long as this plastic, suggestible association of cells remains active? For example, it would appear that although strangers from another like community will be accepted and treated as fellow members, some lack of sympathy, or different habit of work mars the perfection of the building. In renewing the bone structure after trephining, for instance, it has been found that a graft from the patient's own body—thin slices from the tibia are now being used—produces better results than can be achieved by the workers with strange material. The graft in this case is only used as a scaffolding. (Our assumed workers with all their ingenuity are not equal to the task of throwing out cantilevers into the void.) But the planks of the scaffolding become an organic part of the new structure, and when the new material used is foreign, we find the marks of divided purpose in plan and construction. The new bone takes longer to form and the work is not so well done.

(Incidentally, it is interesting to notice how impossible our mechanical metaphors become when we are speaking of this work of the cells. I have spoken of throwing out a cantilever, and incorporating the planks of a scaffold in the new structure, but cantilevers and planks are themselves, also, workers! And, indeed, the fact that the process cannot be truly stated or even conceived in mechanical terms may be taken as a contribution to the metaphysical argument.)

Yet astounding and difficult as is this problem of the civic, corporate life that is being lived without our knowledge, a still more inconceivable partnership awaits our investigation. So far, we have touched only on two domains; the first peculiar to those who study the body from a more or less mechanical aspect, such as the surgeon or the histologist; the second to the psychologist. There remains, I believe, a third peculiar to the practical experiments of biology and psychology.

Such reflections as these have often haunted me, and my mind was confusedly feeling for some key to the whole mystery as I stood by the death-bed of old Henry Sturton. He had been fatally injured by a motor omnibus as he stood in the gutter with his pitiful tray of useless twopenny toys. No one else had been hurt; the accident would have been no accident, nothing more than a violent and harmless skidding of the juggernaut, if Henry Sturton had not been standing on that precise spot. A difference of a few inches either way would have saved him. As it was the whole performance seemed to have been fastidiously planned in order to destroy him. And in his pocket they had found a begging letter addressed to me that he had perhaps forgotten to post. Or it may be that for once he had honestly intended to stamp it? I had egotistically wondered if I was the person for whose benefit this casual killing had been undertaken.

When I reached the hospital, he was either asleep or unconscious, but they allowed me to wait within the loop of the screen that was to hide the spectacle of his passing from the other patients in the ward. And I stood there pondering on the marvel of the bodily functions. I got no further than that until he opened his eyes and I saw my vision.

He had been a gross man. I had always disliked and despised him since a certain occasion on which I had lunched with him at his Club. That was more than twenty years ago. I was young then, full of eagerness for the spiritual adventure of life, and he was a successful business man of nearly fifty, coarse and stupid, drugged by his perpetual indulgence in physical satisfactions. But, indeed, he had always been stupid. He was, I have heard, the typical lout of his school, too lethargic to be vicious, living entirely, as it seemed, for his stomach and his bed. Heaven knows what his life would have been, if he had always been forced to work for his bare living, but Providence has a habit of pandering to fat men, and he succeeded to his father's business, and let it run itself on its own familiar lines.

He had never married. He was too selfish for that, but he had, so someone told me, bought and mistreated more than one young woman for his own office—his only positive sin in the eyes of the moralists; though I used to feel that his whole existence was one vast overwhelming sin from first to last. That, however, is the common error of judgment of the ascetic, self-immolating type.

He found no friends when his business failed. His intimates were men of the same calibre as himself, and rejected him in those circumstances as he would have rejected them. The failure itself was an unlucky accident. The man who ran the business proved unfaithful; he was the victim of a confidence that begot in him the lust for power. He gambled, lost, and absconded.

Sturton's descent into the gutter was delayed for a few years by a clerical appointment he begged from some firm with whom he had traded before his bankruptcy. The appointment could not have been lucrative. He attended the office every day, but nothing else seemed to have been expected of him. He could have been capable of nothing else. Whatever his potentialities may once have been, they were hopelessly stultified by then. I used to meet him now and again in those days of his clerkship; and let him gorge himself at my expense. That was his single pleasure and desire. Poverty had exaggerated the cravings of his gluttony.

And as I stood respectfully within the fold of the screen and looked down at the flabby coarseness of the horrible old man in the bed, I reflected that his body must in its own way have represented a highly successful community of cells. There had been no distractions of purpose in the entity we knew as Henry Sturton; no rending uncertainties to upset his nerves and interfere with the steady industry of his bodily functions.

I was thinking that when he opened his eyes and I caught a glimpse of the fierce and splendid thing his body had always hidden from us. I saw it then, beyond any shadow of doubt—the spirit that had been imprisoned for seventy years, lying in wait eternally patient and vigilant, for this one brief instant of expression. It looked at me without recognition, yet with an amazing intensity, as if it knew that all its long agony of suppression would find no other compensation than this. So near release, his soul, still longing to touch life at some point, had seized its opportunity when that intolerably gross barrier of his body had been mangled and dislocated by this long-delayed accident.

Then Henry Sturton coughed, and I saw the beautiful eager stare die out of his eyes, and give place to that look of gross desire I had always loathed. Even then, I believe, he craved for food. But the next moment his eyes closed and his lips spurted a stream of blood.

The nurse was with him instantly, pushing me aside. I took advantage of her preoccupation to stay till the end. I hoped for one more sight of his soul. I thought it might take advantage of another intermission before the work of the community was abruptly closed. But I did not see it again.

He spoke once, two minutes before he died.

"God blast," was what he said.

THE CONVERT

For the first time in his life, Henry Wolverton had been seriously upset.

His had been an orderly life. Even when he was at Shrewsbury, he had escaped bullying and other disturbances. He had been marked out as a future scholar who would be a credit to the school; and his calm air of reserve had also protected him. He might be classed as a "swat," but he was not the kind of swat who gets singled out for bullying. He was no good at games, but he had a handsome, dignified presence, and he was never known to put on side.

At Oxford he passed from triumph to triumph. After he got his fellowship at Balliol, he married a girl-graduate from Lady Margaret Hall, and they worked happily together on his research. He was writing in many volumes, the Economic History of the Sixteenth & Seventeenth Centuries; and at twenty-nine he was already an authority. His wife died rather incidentally when they had been married three years, but that had not seriously interfered with his life work.

Nor did the war, although it was a terrible nuisance, have any considerable effect upon him. He undertook work of "national importance" in Whitehall, and when he returned home in the afternoon to the house he had taken at the corner of Bedford Square, he found that he could still put in four or five valuable hours' work on his history. And if he wanted extra time for research in the British Museum library, he could always get leave. Everyone in his department recognized the fact that he was an exceptional man, and that the work he was engaged upon would be a lasting monument to English scholarship.

By comparison, the war itself was almost an ephemeral thing.

Since the signing of the armistice, he had settled down to make up for lost time. He had his whole future planned. He hoped to finish his immediate task by the time he was sixty-five, but he foresaw that there would still be other work for him to do. He would, for example, almost certainly find it necessary by then to make revision in his earlier volumes.

It was no trifle that had upset him on this particular day. But even the fact that the English revolution had at last broken into the flame of civil war would not have disturbed him so seriously, if he had not conclusively proved in the course of the past five weeks that the revolution was impossible. Throughout the welter of the national strike disturbances, editors of any importance from the editor of the Times downwards had begged him for articles. Although he had specialized upon a study of the sixteenth and seventeenth centuries, he was regarded as the first authority on the entire history of the English people. And in his articles, he had proved conclusively from his vast knowledge of precedents and tradition, that the temper of the English people would never seek the arbitrament of an armed revolution.

He was still convinced of that, although, so far as he could judge, the revolution had already begun.

He had been startled in the middle of his best hours of the day, by what he had at first imagined to be the back-firing of a rapidly driven motor-bicycle. He went to the window, opened it wide (he always kept it closed when he was working, to shut out the noise of the traffic), and listened with an anxious attention. He had a peculiar and unprecedented feeling of nervousness. He felt, for no assignable reason, as if someone had discovered a bad anachronism in his book. And then he was reluctantly driven to the conclusion that, indeed, some mistake had been committed, although he could not admit that it was his own. For the motor-bicycle continued to back-fire in short, spasmodic bursts, while it remained stationary; and he could do longer avoid the inference that it was as a matter of fact a machine gun, no further away than Oxford Street. He could, also, hear dim and terrible shouting, and more faintly, occasional cries of dismay, of anger, or of fear.

The Square was completely deserted, but when he saw a scattered rout of people flying north, up Bloomsbury Street, he closed the window and began to pace up and down his well-fitted writing room, sanctified now, by the five years' work he had done there.

What so annoyed and disturbed him was that some officious, political fool should have upset his scholarly deductions from the vast precedents of history. He would not admit for one moment that he had been mistaken; his chain of reasoning was unassailable. But, so he inferred, some blundering, malicious idiot had made a gross error in the conduct of the negotiations that, no longer ago than yesterday, had promised so hopefully. The result of that error was incalculable. There could be no doubt that the rioters had been fired upon, and so given a sound cause, and what would perhaps be more effective still, a rallying cry, to the great mass of unemployed workers. And the army could not be depended upon. The more loyal part of it was in Germany enforcing the peace terms. It was just possible in the circumstances that there might be something very like an armed revolution, despite the fact that his arguments had been so indubitably sound and right. Henry Wolverton was exceedingly annoyed and upset.

His troubles did not end there. Just as he had succeeded, by a masterly effort of concentration, in putting away the thought of this stupid anomaly and returning to his work, his housekeeper came and tapped at his door—a thing she had been explicitly forbidden to do, at that time of day, in any circumstances whatever.

He ignored the first knock, and then she knocked again, more loudly.

He frowned, and bade her come in. She was stupid, like most women, and would probably continue to pester him until she was admitted.

She came in trembling with agitation.

"Oh! I'm sure I beg your pardon, sir, coming now, against all orders," she said; "but William has just come in—it's his evening off, you know, sir—and he says there's been firin' in Oxford Circus, and people killed, and—"

"I inferred that," Henry Wolverton interrupted her calmly. "I heard the machine guns. You had better tell William not to go out again."

"Oh! sir, but he says we're none of us safe," the housekeeper wailed, on the verge of hysterics. "He says there'll be looting and Heaven only knows what, and us so near Oxford Street."

"I do not anticipate any effects of that kind, to-night, Mrs. Perry," Wolverton replied frigidly. "And, by the way, I should be glad if you could let me have dinner half an hour earlier, this evening. After these annoying disturbances, I may not be able to settle down again until I have dined, and I shall work longer afterwards to make up for lost time. Can you arrange that?"

"Yes, sir," gasped Mrs. Perry. "Then, you don't believe, sir—"

"I do not," Wolverton returned with the dignity of the assured. "You may lock the outer doors, if it gives you any sense of security. I shall expect dinner in half an hour from now."

Mrs. Perry returned to the kitchen greatly comforted by her master's magnificent confidence. She told William that things were not so bad as he was afraid of! And William in his turn derived a sense of security from the knowledge that he was living in the house of Henry Wolverton.

Nevertheless, they locked and bolted all the doors with a fine attention to detail.

Henry Wolverton worked rather intermittently after dinner that night. He was not disturbed by any noises from without. London was quieter than he had ever known it. He could hear no sound of traffic either along Bloomsbury Street or Tottenham Court Road. No paper boys came. No one passed his window. He could not even hear the sound of the policeman on his beat. But he found the absence of noise on this occasion more disturbing than the presence of it would have been. He found himself hailed out of his profoundest efforts of attention by his consciousness of this abiding, deathly silence. He would discover himself, sitting idly, listening to the stillness of the night.

A little after twelve o'clock, he got up and went to the front door. And after he had somewhat impatiently unlocked it, drawn back the bottom bolt and the top bolt, released the night latch, and undone the chain, he opened the door and stood on the top step, looking out over the darkness of the Square. After a moment or two, he realized with a little shock of dismay why the Square looked unfamiliar to him. The street lamps had not been lighted. Only a clear and brilliant moon in its second quarter, brooded over the unprecedented silence; weakly illuminating the apparently deserted city....

The thin scream of fear that suddenly pierced the stillness, came with an effect of audacious irreverence.

Henry Wolverton stiffened and a cold thrill of apprehension ran down his spine.

The scream was succeeded by a faint, eager patter of hurrying feet; and then more distantly, by the brutal intrusion of hoarse shouts, and the clutter of heavy boots vehemently running.

Wolverton did not move. Until now fear had never entered his life and he had the courage of a man who has never faced a real danger.

The lighter footsteps were approaching very rapidly, coming up Bloomsbury Street; and the sound of them seemed suddenly to lift and acquire precision as a figure came round the corner and turned swiftly into the Square. Wolverton could see then that the runner was a young woman in a light dress.

He would have let her pass without trying to attract her attention. He was watching the whole incident with the detached and careful interest of the historian. But the young woman, herself, had evidently seen the beacon of his open door before she actually reached it, and had settled upon her course of action. She came straight up the steps without an instant's hesitation, pushed Henry Wolverton back into the hall, and closed the door with the intent and silent urgency of a conspirator.

He made no attempt to speak, and the young woman crouched in silence behind the door, until they had heard the clutter of heavy footsteps pass by and hurry on, up the Square. The men were not shouting now, but even through the heavy door, Wolverton could hear them gasping and panting as they ran. The sound of it made him think of the hoarse panting of great dogs.

When the flurry of that passing had dwindled again into silence, the young woman got up, locked and bolted the door and faced Henry Wolverton under the light of the hall lamp.

"So, that's all right," she said, with a little laugh of exultation.

"Do I understand—?" Wolverton began.

"Probably, I should imagine," she interrupted him. "The scum's let loose—the hooligans; the Apaches. After the fighting comes pillage and rapine." She frowned slightly as she added, "I suppose rapine has got to do with rape?"

"It is not used specifically in that sense, now," Wolverton replied. "But it had that meaning, earlier."

"Oh, thanks! Well that was what I meant," the young woman said. "Do you mind if I come in and sit down? Is that your room? I'm a bit blown."

Wolverton stood aside for her to enter the sacred places of his writing-room.

She nodded by way of thanks, as she passed him, went in, looked round the room and then having thrown herself with a sigh of relief into his reading chair, proceeded to take off her hat.

"Jolly room," she remarked pleasantly, as her deft fingers twitched and patted at her hair. "You a writer?"

"My name is Henry Wolverton," he informed her with a modest dignity.

"What?" she exclaimed, sitting bolt upright and staring at him eagerly. "Henry Wolverton, the historian?"

He nodded gravely.

"Oh, Lord!" she said, and went on, "Well, I was wrong about one thing. I said you must be a dried up little mummy of a man, all beard and spectacles. And you're not a bit like that. In fact you're quite unusually goodlooking."

The faintest adumbration of a flush tinged Wolverton's white forehead. "My name appears to be known to you," he remarked, ignoring the compliment.

"Obviously," his visitor retorted. "Pretty well known to everyone, I should imagine, just now."

"May I ask why?" he put in.

"Well, considering that you're the man who's responsible for the revolution, I suppose you're more famous at the present moment than any man in Great Britain," she said. "Though you're not exactly popular with either side, to-night, I should think," she added thoughtfully.

Henry Wolverton made a little noise in his throat that sounded like an asthmatic cough. With him that noise did duty for a laugh. "I'm afraid I don't follow you," he said.

"Do you mean that you don't admit your own responsibility for the revolution?" she asked.

"I cannot see that I am even remotely connected with it," he replied.

The young woman pursed her lovely mouth, and clasped her hands round her knee. After a reflective pause she remarked with apparent inconsequence, "My name is Susan Jeffery; but I don't suppose that conveys anything to you."

"I believe I saw the name on a committee list of the 'League of Youth,'" Wolverton said.

"Lord, what a memory he has," commented Susan Jeffery in a soft voice.

"But I must plead ignorance of the general scope of your activities," he continued.

"But you know something about our league?" she put in.

"Something," he admitted.

"Such as our policy of percolation?"

"I understand that your endeavour is to be represented in every imaginable grade of society."

"Precisely. From royalty down to the criminal and the gutter-snipe," Susan confirmed. "We have only one qualification for membership; we admit no one over twenty-five."

"And have you many members, now?" Wolverton inquired politely.

"Nine thousand, eight hundred and forty-three," Susan replied. "We admitted a hundred and seven new members after our grand meeting to-night, including a royal prince and two hooligans."

Henry Wolverton nodded his head encouragingly.

"Most satisfactory," he murmured.

Susan dropped her knee and sat up.

"I'm telling you this," she said in a firm voice, "for your own good. We discussed you at our meeting, and it was resolved unanimously that you were largely responsible for the revolution that broke out to-day, and will end God knows where or when."

Wolverton made his noise again—Susan had not yet recognized it as a laugh. "I must confess that I don't quite follow your train of reasoning," he said.

"You don't look like a fool, either," Susan commented, frankly. "I suppose that's just your one blind spot. Most of us have one."

"Perhaps you would explain," Wolverton suggested.

"It's so bally obvious," Susan replied. "You've been writing articles for the last six weeks—they've appeared all over the shop—rubbing it in about the English temper. It wouldn't have mattered if it had been anybody else, but people believe you. All sorts of people. We know that, through the activities of the league, because we're represented everywhere. Well, what has been the effect of those articles? One side, the side in power, has believed you and decided on your authority not to give way. The other side, the workers, has believed you, too, and they're so annoyed to think that you are right that they've determined to prove you're wrong."

"But, in that case, I was right," Wolverton put in with his first sign of excitement.

"You were, until you put your opinion on record," Susan corrected him. "You see," she explained, "it's like knowing the future. You can only know it for certain about other people as long as you keep it to yourself. If you tell a man that next Friday he'll walk under a ladder in Fleet Street, and that a brick will drop on his head and kill him, he'll keep out of Fleet Street next Friday, if he believes you."

"I admit the instance," Wolverton murmured.

"Well, it's just the same in your case. The workers have been saying, 'Here's that chap Wolverton convincing everybody that there'll be no revolution, that we'll have to give in, in the end, and make terms. And all the politicians, and the owners and the middle classes believe him, and they'll stick it out to the last minute, because they're sure we have got the "English temper" and won't fight. Well, we'll jolly well prove that Mr. Wolverton is wrong for once.' You see," Susan concluded with a graceful gesture. "Our league knows these things. And it comes to this: if you want your prophecies to come off, you must keep them to yourself until after the event. Hasn't your study of history taught you that much?"

Henry Wolverton leaned forward in his chair and covered his face with his hands.

"I'm sorry if I've upset you," Susan said gently. "I'm sure you're a very nice man, really."

Wolverton groaned. "I'm finally discredited," he muttered.

"Oh, no!" Susan comforted him. "Not in your own line. Remember the motto of our League: 'These things are hidden from the wise and prudent and revealed unto babes.' No man, however clever he is, can be expected to know everything."

Henry Wolverton lifted his head.

"I shall never write again," he said, in the tone of one who makes the great renunciation; and he looked at Susan a trifle nervously, as if he feared this immense announcement might be a little too much for her.

"Just as well," she replied soothingly. "In any case we've pretty well scrapped history now. It was never any practical use except as a reference for precedents; and now we're chucking precedents down the sink as fast as we can. We're all going to begin again presently—when the fighting is over—on a new basis."

Henry Wolverton jumped to his feet and began to pace up and down the room.

"It's sure to be a wrench at first, of course," Susan consoled him. "These things always are. But if I can help you in any way—"

He turned on her with the first sign of emotional passion he had ever displayed.

"You!" he said fiercely. "Don't you realize that you've destroyed my whole life's work; that you've robbed me in ten minutes of every happiness and satisfaction I've ever had. Good God, if I'd known, I'd have slammed the door in your face, just now. I would have delivered you over to the scum of London to do what they would with you."

Susan blushed. "I don't think that's a very nice thing to say," she remarked, gently. "But perhaps it's just as well for you to blow off steam a bit. It does help when you've had a real facer. And honestly, you know, although I'm very sorry in a way, I do think it's all for your good that I came in to-night; because you would have been bound to find it out for yourself sooner or later."

Henry Wolverton stared at her, and his look of anger slowly gave place to one of bewilderment.

"But what am I to do?" he asked. "I've always worked for ten hours a day. I can't live without work of some kind, and now...."

Susan got up and came across the room to him, with an expression of bright and eager helpfulness.

"Oh! look here, we'll find a use for you," she said, laying her hand on his arm. "You're too old to join the league, of course—"

"I'm thirty-seven," he interpolated.

"It's quite young, really," she comforted him. "I'm twenty-three. But what I was going to say was that we are founding a reference committee of experts of all kinds to advise the league. The members of that committee will have no voice in our decisions, you understand; they'll be simply advisory. And it would be absolutely splendid to have you as chairman. I shall get no end of prestige from the league for having found you." Her face shone with the joy of the successful discoverer.

"I understand you to suggest," Henry Wolverton commented dryly, "that I should devote the rest of my life, and the—er—fruits of my scholarship, to instructing young men and women under twenty-five years of age in the lessons of history; always with the distinct understanding that they are in no way pledged to apply my advice in the prosecution of their own policy?"

Susan did not miss the implications of his tone. "My dear man," she said, "whatever is the good of scholarship, if it isn't to advise the young? Surely you haven't been studying history all these years just in order to swap opinions with all the other old fogies?"

Henry Wolverton turned his back on her and walked over to the window. After a short pause he faced her again and said, "You have a remarkable power of statement, Miss Jeffery. I must admit that I have never before considered the precise use, in the pragmatical sense, to which I might apply my—er—scholarship; and I am ready to grant that your point is a good one. Where your otherwise admirable logic seems to fail, however, is in the admission that though I might turn my knowledge to good effect by advising youth, I may be wasting all my effort since youth will probably not be guided by my teaching."

"I don't know much about logic," replied Susan, "but I should have thought it must be pretty evident to you, to-day of all days, that if we were going to be guided only by the lessons of history, our league would be a back-number in a week. Isn't it possible for you to get it into your head that history isn't everything?"

She put her last question with the appealing gesture of a mother addressing a refractory and rather stupid child.

"How is history going to get us out of the mess you've landed us in, for example?" she continued, as Henry Wolverton made no attempt to answer her. "How is history, alone, going to help us presently to start everything afresh on a new basis? You must know, yourself, that it's no good trying to get back to the old way of doing things. That could only mean, by your own showing, that we should just be preparing the way for all this to happen again."

Henry Wolverton threw up his hands with a gesture of despair.

"But if I admit that you're right," he said, "I have to face the conclusion that I've wasted my whole life."

"Well, in a way, I'm afraid you have, rather," Susan admitted. "It's a great pity, for instance, about this revolution of yours. It means such a lot of blood and disorder; and people do get so out of hand when there's fighting going on. Now if the owners and the middle-classes hadn't been so cocksure, and had given way, we could have started in on our new methods of government without any bother."

She paused a moment, before she added,

"We've got it all worked out, you know, but, of course, I can't tell you anything about it, yet."

"I am, in fact, what you would call a back-number," Henry Wolverton said.

Susan puckered her forehead. "I think there's still a hope for you," she remarked.

"After all these years?" he asked.

"If you'd let me take you in hand for a bit," she said. "You seem willing to learn."

"But you have surely more important work to do? You couldn't spare time to teach me?" he suggested.

"I think I might work it in," she said reflectively. "I'd take you about with me and show you things—real things, you know. What's chiefly wrong with you is that you've spent all your time over your old books."

"You suggest that I ought to study life in—in action?" Henry Wolverton inquired.

"Rather," Susan agreed. "You ought to come to one of our meetings."

She stopped abruptly, and her hand went up to her mouth with a gesture of dismay.

"Oh! Great Scott!" she ejaculated; "that reminds me, I was going on to another frightfully important meeting when those hooligans started chasing me; and that and our talk put it right out of my head."

"At what time was this important meeting to be held?" Henry Wolverton asked, looking at his watch.

"One o'clock," she told him.

"You still have ten minutes," he said.

Susan shuddered. "I daren't go out again alone," she confessed. "I simply daren't. I'd—I'd sooner stay here all night with you."

"I shall be delighted to come with you," Henry Wolverton said.

"You!" Susan exclaimed. "But don't you understand the risk? The mob's loose. What good would you be against three or four chunky hooligans?"

Henry Wolverton squared his shoulders. He was a tall, finely-built man, and his face had the cool assurance of one who has never known fear.

"I am not afraid of hooligans," he said.

Susan gazed at him with frank admiration.

"You know you're a perfect topper in some ways," she complimented him.

He bowed gravely. "If I might be admitted to this meeting of yours," he said; "it would perhaps afford me an opportunity to begin my education."

"If you're sure you're not afraid," Susan replied, picking up her hat.

"I'm not in the least afraid," he said. "Will you take my arm?"

At the open door they paused a moment, looking out into the darkness; listening to the profound silence of the empty night—creative youth and patient scholarship, hand-in-hand, facing the immense void of the unforetellable future.

A NEGLIGIBLE EXPERIMENT

"I can't get him right, somehow," the young sculptor said, but he looked tenderly at the little figure of the man he was modelling in plasticine, as if, despite its very obvious defects, he found something to admire in his creation.

"Wants stiffening, doesn't he?" I suggested. "Couldn't you put a wire or something up his legs and back?"

"Well, you see," my young friend explained, "I could if I knew beforehand exactly what I was going to do with him. Only I don't. I like to make him up as I go along. I'm no good at it really. I can't think it all out ahead and then sit down and do it right off. I have to experiment and—see how it comes, you know. Do you think his head is too big?"

I thought it was rather big.

The young modeller regarded his creation with a look in which fondness still seemed to preponderate.

"Perhaps if...." he said; then speech died out of him as his hands again began to fashion and improve his little image of humanity.

And as I watched him a vision came to me. I lost consciousness of the boy and his workshop. I wandered away into a dreamland of the imagination, following the lure of a fantasy deeper and more satisfying than the reality of life.

When I read in my morning's paper of the "Nova" in the constellation of Sagittarius, I thought first of H. G. Wells's story of "The New Star," and smiled. Later, I turned with a little shiver of anxiety to that chapter in Professor Lowell's Evolution of Worlds in which he describes the possible coming of a "dark stranger" out of the depths of space. Already there were points of striking resemblance between Lowell's imaginative account and the details that were appearing casually, in the intervals between more important news, in the newspapers. This new star differed from those other novæ so many of which have been recorded at various times. They brought us tidings of a collision that had already occurred, blazing out suddenly into a short-lived splendour and quickly waning again to invisibility. This stranger, astronomers were agreed, shone not by its own light but by the reflected light of the sun. Then it must be, relatively, near. Lowell's calculations gave us something like thirty years to prepare before the invader wrought the destruction of the solar system. But, obviously, that calculation depended on various assumptions that the reality need not verify. This strange visitor might be much smaller than he had assumed—he had taken the enormous mass of the sun as his standard—its albedo might be lower; its speed greater. Also Lowell's stranger was assumed to be coming at right angles to the plane of the ecliptic; this one would, as it were, skim the edge of that swimming saucer. Would any of the outer planets be interposed between us and this dreadful visitor? Neptune, Uranus, Saturn, Jupiter, Mars, might any of them be a buffer to us—provide us, perhaps, with some stupendous display in the heavens, but save us from ultimate disaster?

Everyone treated the thing so lightly. Here and there alarmist paragraphs appeared, but they only displayed the hand of the sensation-monger. No one took the threat seriously. And yet the astronomers must know? They had had more than a week, now, in which to make their calculations.

And then the shadow fell with such suddenness that it was impossible to say how the certainty had come to us. Everyone knew. The astronomers confirmed one another without a dissentient. And there was nothing in the way. With a horrible unanimity the outer planets had left a clear space for the intruder, while the Earth, with that blundering indifference which is surely its chief characteristic, was stolidly marching straight into the path of destruction. Is there any esoteric significance in the fact that the Earth has a greater density than any other member of the solar system?

Everyone knew, but little was changed. We went on with our affairs; with little zest, no doubt—we could never forget the deepening shadow. But what else was there for us to do but go on? We could not instantly alter ourselves or our way of life. Religions blazed into a spasmodic fever as men and women sought refuge from the dreadful reality. Crimes of lust and greed increased for the same reason. But for the most part we continued in the old ways by sheer inertia, though there was a new and smaller moon visible to us in the night sky, a moon that waxed with infinite slowness towards the full, and grew larger night by night. We knew by then that the stranger was as big as Jupiter, and with a density little less than that of the Earth.

The first portents of disaster came when our own moon was approaching the new. The stranger's mass had begun to affect the tides, and we were warned to evacuate all low lands, near the sea, upon the estuaries, and incidentally the river level in London. Four days before the highest tide the Thames flooded Farringdon Street, Westminster, and great districts on the south bank, and the retreating river laid bare the river-bed as far down as Greenwich.

The population of London had fled to the heights North and South before the great floods that devastated all the low lands of Essex, Kent, Surrey, and Middlesex. And with that rush for safety and the rapidly increasing portents of disaster the routine of civilisation was definitely broken. It seemed as if in the mass we were being gradually stripped of all our tediously-acquired virtues and vices, until but one instinct remained, the instinct for self-preservation. That, however, was only the effect produced by the panic movement of the crowd; when one came to individuals....

I can, however, only speak of two, myself and another man. We sat together on a hill in Derbyshire and watched through the last night.

A certain calmness had come to me, then, mingled with the queerest feelings of excitement and expectation. Within sight of death, I could still enjoy this amazing celestial adventure. The new planet that was rushing in upon us had already torn us from our steady path about the sun, and our old familiar moon dwindled to the size of a sixpence, and, diminishing almost visibly, was within a few hours of destruction. For the moon had fled its old allegiance to the Earth and was rushing to the arms of this great stranger like some passionate, unfaithful lover.

But the new planet itself drowned all consciousness of lesser things when it rose magnificently above the eastern horizon. That night it was a full circle of yellow light, and across its great expanse moved one circle of intense blackness, the size of our old moon, a circle that was slowly increasing in size, the shadow of our own Earth. So great a thing appeared this new planet, then, that when its lower rim was at last clear of the horizon, its upper limb towered half-way to the zenith. It had few markings, but from one pole, which was turned markedly towards us, radiated uneven, dark lines—chains of mountains, perhaps—that definitely produced the effect of a solid globe long before its actual convexity was recognisable. All the rest of the planet presented a smooth, unbroken expanse, possibly the vast bed of some long-vanished sea.

For an hour or more my companion and I had sat in silence watching this gigantic spectacle; then he said quietly, "We are witnessing the failure of a negligible experiment."

I did not answer at once. I had not caught his drift. I was struggling with a foolish preoccupation, the result of an almost lifelong habit. As I watched I was searching for words to describe what I saw. I wanted to write my experience; yes, even there, under the sentence of death pronounced not only upon me, but upon all humanity, I was struggling with this meaningless desire to create a record that none could ever read.

I made an effort and roused myself from this inane preoccupation. "Negligible?" I said, grasping at what seemed to be his most prominent word.

"Proved to be negligible," he asserted. "You are a serious man? You don't cling to straws? You have no doubt that this is the end of the Earth? Very well then, you know that we are to be destroyed? By an accident? Possibly. Or it may be that this arrow that has been discharged at us was shot deliberately; with a definite purpose.

"It isn't as if the same thing had not happened before," he continued after a pause. "We have seen it—seen the effects at least. When some temporary star blazed up in the sky, we inferred some such collision as this. It may very well be that from a planet in some other system men may catch sight of this tiny blaze of ours—and wonder. It will be relatively a very small affair. Some of those we've seen must have been many thousand times greater.

"But the point is that this experiment of making men upon the Earth is now proved to be negligible. In a few hours it will be finished, wiped out. And whether that termination is the result of accident or design makes no difference to the effect. This is an answer to all our philosophies and religions. Either we are the creatures of some chance evolutionary process, or we are an experiment that has failed."

I looked at him, and noted with a curious stir of unplaceable recollection that his head was too large.

"It is certain that we shall go off like an exploded shell?" I asked.

"I don't fancy that many of us will live to see that," he replied. "Most of us will be drowned in the next tide. It will come in a wall of water many thousand feet high. Don't you notice a feeling of lightness in your body? The attraction of this great stranger is beginning to drag at us. On the other side of the Earth men are feeling an intolerable heaviness. And our speed increases. We have been drawn out of our orbit. We are rushing now to greet the stranger with a kiss of fire. Our circling about the sun is done for ever. We and the stranger are leaping together like two bubbles in a cup."

I believe some hours passed before I spoke again. A sense of imminence had grown upon me in the meantime. I was aware of the guards that were fetching me to execution.

"After all," I cried, "there may still be such a thing as an immortal soul. Though every physical expression is smashed at one blow, that does not prove...."

"There is no such thing as proof possible," my companion interrupted. "But don't you know in your heart that it's no good?"

"No good. It's no good." I woke with a start at the repetition of that statement.

My young modeller was rolling a great ball of plasticine, and before I could stop him he had thrown it with deadly accuracy at his effigy of man.

"He wouldn't come right," he explained, picked up the shapeless mass of clay, and tossed it carelessly into a corner of the workshop.

"Oh, but you shouldn't have done that," I said, with the incurable didacticism of the pedagogue.

THE MIRACLE

"I'm dead."

She heard the voice, his voice, speaking distinctly, with something of the same fatalism, half-careless, half-resentful, that he had used when he returned to France after their five short days of married life. For one moment she believed that it was actually his voice, that he had come suddenly and wonderfully out of his six weeks' insensibility, to a doubting interrogation of the darkness. But even as she fumbled impatiently for the switch of the electric light, she knew that the voice had not come from the bed on the further side of the room, but had spoken its horrible message close, very close, to her ear—intimately, confidentially, with a touch of swaggering, careless courage.

And as the light, with an effect of servile obedience, disclosed the room at her touch of the switch, she had no least hope that she would be the witness of the longed-for miracle; that she would see him who had lain so long a lax and useless counterfeit of his vigorous self, half raised and questioning the unfamiliar surroundings with his pitiful assertion.

Nevertheless she got out of bed, a slight pathetic figure in the white light that searched out every corner of the room, and crossed to where he lay inert and flaccid.

No, there was no change in him. The enigma that had baffled all the specialists still persisted. He was still the living dead man who had been ejected with just one little sobbing gasp of air out of the narrow tunnel, the bore of his own body, by the premature explosion of the mine he had spent six weeks' labour in laying. On the further side that explosion had blown out the flank of a hill, but he who had stoppered the narrow vent on the hither side, like a plug of damp earth in the mouth of a rifle-barrel, had been softly expelled into the presence of his fellow-sappers waiting at the junction of the wider tunnel they had bored, with never a mark of injury on him. Even his hair, which had been so near—a paltry twenty feet or so—to the charge that had lifted goodness knows how many tons of earth and stone sky-high—even his hair had not been singed.

His body, almost incredibly, had come unscathed from its open sight of death, but something—his wife thought of it as his spirit—had been instantly shocked into silence. Since that awful experience he had given no sign of consciousness or of volition. His bodily functions continued their offices with a slow, dull persistence—he was fed artificially now and again to remedy the slight waste of tissue—but his spirit gave no least sign of its occupancy.

The specialists had been greatly interested, but he had given them so little material for actual experiment that they had yielded to his wife's urgent request, and yesterday he had been transferred to her immediate care in the reasonably convenient Maida Vale flat in which they had spent their too restricted honeymoon....

She leant over him now and stared into his composed impassive face, every feature of which was steady with the challenging quiet of death. Where was he? she wondered. What could she conceivably do to reach him through that unresponsive instrument on the bed—an instrument that appeared as useless now as an unstrung piano?

And the voice, that had made its immense admission with the desperate gallantry of one who had flung up his arms and acknowledged himself prisoner to the great enemy—whence had come the voice? She could remember no antecedent dream. The sound of his speaking had wakened her, and in the act of waking she had heard his surrender made, as clearly as if he had spoken it with his mouth at her ear. She felt that she could hear it still. That reckless sentence was yet ringing through the room: "I'm dead." Just so, she thought, might he have said "Kamerad" in face of some overwhelmingly superior force.

"But you're not; you're not dead," she pleaded to that insensible figure; "you're alive if—if you would but come back."

She might as well have strummed on the keyboard of a wireless piano for all the reaction she could produce from the lax representative that lay before her, but her own verbal image returned to her with another question.

Come back? From where? Where was he now—the individuality she addressed as "you"? Was that essential personality of his buried deep in this spiritless automaton, or was it away somewhere in the void, unaware both of its fleshly anchor and of her? Could she not reach that spirit of his, poised out of time and space, by the powers of her own love and longing, since they, too, surely were able to transcend the limitations of the purely physical? But to do that she must not sit and gaze at this empty replica on the bed; she must think not of his image, but of him, not of the representative, but of the spirit.

Nevertheless, when she began to pace the length of the room, she found that when the sight of her husband's placid face was hidden some stimulus to concentration was removed also. While she stared at him her thought was held and focused, now she was distracted by her vision of the familiar things that were associated with her past life in his company. She was thinking, not of him, but of the things he had done, the man he had been.

Perhaps darkness might help her, she thought, and she laid herself down on the bed and once more quenched the obedient light.

For a time she lay still, staring into the blackness, clenched in a vivid effort of concentration, and then her eyes closed, and even as she protested that she would not sleep, she had a vision of herself lying inert and pale on her own bed, even as he was lying.

Then she seemed to be rising, baffled and half-unwilling, through wreaths of a palpable darkness that clung about her with a dragging, suffocating weight. And then it seemed to her that she was wandering, lost and perplexed, on a gaunt and arid plain that might once have been the bed of a now vanished sea.

She was not alone. Other figures, wraiths of humanity, also wandered here and there. But none noticed her. They moved as if they were searching for something they could never hope to find. They peered vaguely downwards, passing her with bent heads and eyes that sought the ground with a reluctant determination....

She found herself trembling, not with horror, but with a rapture of expectancy. She had become aware that one among these drifting wraiths was moving definitely towards her, drawn by the power of her longing. And she had command of the power, so that it was ecstasy to wield it. Almost she was tempted to withhold her amazing strength in order to taste again the pleasure of its renewed exercise.

Then with a sense of some lost interval she found herself face to face with him. But he looked at her without a sign of recognition. His eyes, too, were full of that aimless intention, as though he was under an eternal command to search for some unknown thing that was hidden he knew not where.

"Paul!" she cried to him.

He made no reply. He did not seem to have heard her. But still she was conscious of her immense power over him.

"Paul," she said again. "Come back with me."

He heard her then; but now it was as if he could not see her. He looked about him, half-startled, half-resentful. "There's no way back from the plains of France," he said, and a sudden doubt shook her. Her power to hold him was failing. From out of the ground the darkness was rising again like a swelling lake of still, black smoke, clinging about her feet with an awful weight of recall.

She was sinking into the blackness, struggling against its vast strength as it rose, sluggish and irresistible, to her waist, her breast, her neck. She could not fight its immense strength, but her power had returned to her. They might be drowned together in the darkness, but she would compel him to come with her. She could see him no longer, but she was aware of her limitless ability to hold him to her by the power of her longing and her love....

She came slowly out of some remote distance to a realisation of herself lying unaccountably still and dazed on her own bed. She could not move, as yet, but her eyes were open, and she could see the grey outline of the room in the growing daylight.

And then, again, clearly, but more distantly, she heard the sound of Paul's voice repeating his strange assertion.

"I'm dead," he said, but in the tone there was now, she thought, the first flicker of a doubt, the statement of wonder.

She made a great effort and raised herself.

He was sitting up in bed, propping his weakened body on his tremulous arms.

"You're not dead, Paul; you're not, you're not," she screamed. "I've brought you back, and I am going to hold you here."

In a moment she was kneeling by him, supporting, clasping him. Her power had become overwhelming, illimitable.

He looked at her with a grin, that was in some way sheepish, a little ashamed.

"Well, if I'm not, I jolly well ought to be," he said.

It must have seemed to him so boastful to be alive again.

No doubt the story of the future is written, so far as the future is an expression of present potentialities. We boast our foreknowledge of planetary history, and can prophesy with fine accuracy the occurrence of every major and minor eclipse or occultation in the solar system. But in the most precise science there remains always at least one element that is undefinable and unknowable. The regular traffic of planets about the sun might one day be upset by the coming of an unknown visitor from the deeps of space. The materials of our knowledge are so limited. And in human affairs we know so little of the materials. Nevertheless, it may be that to the universal consciousness the future is a foretellable expression of our present potentialities.

I remember how my friend Strickland used to harp on that theme eighteen years ago. I was incredulous; a stickler for free-will. I could not bear the thought of anything like a cut-and-dried programme of human development. But my one really convincing retort to all his arguments was to reply, "Oh; on broad lines, perhaps. On the very broadest lines."

Strickland's attitude just then was so obviously influenced by his desires. He had married at forty, had one child, a boy, and was oppressed by the fear that he would not live to see his son's future. Strickland was obsessed with that idea for a time. He even went so far as to consult mediums. And a man of forty-five who will consult professional mediums about the future cannot be quite sane.

His sole excuse for that lapse was the plea that astrology had failed him. He had had two very expensive horoscopes cast, and they had been most grievously at fault concerning the first three years of little Strickland's life. Both forecasts had been gloomy with regard to those early years, prophesying a delicate constitution, unusual trouble with infantile complaints. And one horoscope shrugged its inspired shoulders at the critical period of teething, and continued with a kind of cynical despair, as if the astrologer were a little ashamed of the way he was earning his ten guineas: "Should he, however, survive...." And the truth was that little Strickland was quite a fatiguingly healthy child. His appetite and his craving for exercise, even at the age of eight weeks, were, admittedly, almost abnormal.

So Strickland lost faith in the pattern of the stars, and tried mediums, who were not so nervous of the magistrates in those days. If he had stuck to one clairvoyante he might have laid his restless enquiry, but, unhappily, the first lady he visited misread her client's hopes, and mapped out a successful business career for his little son; and Strickland, who had already fulfilled that destiny in his own life, and had ambitions to see his son leading a "really sensible Government," took another opinion. The second prophetess, pathetically anxious to please, no doubt, saw young Strickland as a Bishop; the third was a shade nearer to the mark with an Admiral; but the fourth—a charming young woman, recently engaged to be married, and collecting a trousseau by her last professional efforts—made the boy a Poet.

After that Strickland bought a crystal, and tried to see the future for himself.

I laughed at him then, of course; and even now I feel inclined to laugh at those first foolish enquiries of his. But his very earnestness should have saved Strickland from anything like ridicule; and I am glad to remember that I did not laugh when he told me of the one and only vision that came to him through the crystal—it was, by the way, an unusually fine specimen, as big as an orange. He picked it up second-hand, somewhere in Soho.

As I see it, one of the most intriguing features of Strickland's experience is the fact that he had ceased to probe his son's future when the vision came. The boy was seven years old then, and had a little sister of two and a half who had partly diverted her father's attention. And Strickland had probably outgrown the fear of his own premature death; though it may be that his passionate longing for assurance as to the glory of his boy's career had not so much spent itself as been thrust back into his sub-consciousness. Superficially the difference in him was quite obvious. The change of his tone, for example, when he spoke of his son. Even the manner of reference. The tender enunciation of "My little boy" had altered to "That young rascal of mine," just the proudly modest description of the ordinary father.

And when the vision came, neither he nor I related it in any way to his ancient search....

He came to my rooms one evening after dinner, produced the crystal from his pocket, and tossed it over to me.

"A present for a sceptic," he said. "I've finished with it."

I might have thought that he was clearing up the lumber of his old fancies if it had not been for his manner; but the garment of his initiation still clung to him and affected me with the strangeness of its mystery.

I shuddered.

"What did you see?" I asked.

"Oh! don't say you believe in it," he said; "after all your jeers at me."

"Did you see anything?" I insisted, nursing the crystal in the cave of my two hands. I stared into it and saw the faint pink of my magnified palm. No vision came to me; yet I was aware of some potency in the thing.

"Perhaps some reflection, some translation of one's sub-consciousness...." I ventured.

Strickland sneered. "By God, I hope not," he said.

"What were you—looking for?" I asked.

"For nothing. I wasn't looking for anything," he said. "I picked the thing up by the merest accident. I was going to give it to the little girl—as a plaything."

"And then...." I prompted him.

"I saw a picture in it. It snatched my attention. I wasn't thinking...."

"And the picture?"

"Hell. Just hell. The real thing; none of your picturesque flames and torture. It came out at me, as it were, and it was—well, the abomination of desolation, nothing more nor less than that."

"But...." I began.

He interrupted me. His eyes were fixed on the vision of a future that had become a fragment of his past. "A waste," he said, in a low, thoughtful voice. "A dead, horrible waste ... all black and pitted and furrowed ... it looked as if there had been some awful, blasting eruption ... or as if the whole earth had been scorched and blighted by some unimaginably vast fire. But, oh! the terrible gauntness and death of it all."

He paused and threw his head back with a queer laugh before he continued in a new tone, "It was just a silly nightmare, that's all. And it had its inevitable element of the grotesque. In the middle of that waste there was a scarecrow, a live scarecrow—digging. Digging turnips, if you please. Oh! it was bosh, of course, absolute bosh. I shall have forgotten all about it next week. But I couldn't give the crystal to the little girl after that. You can keep it. Tell me if you get anything...."

So I kept the crystal, and sometimes stared into it. But no vision came to me.

It was in the late autumn of 1919 that Strickland got permission to go out to France. The war had made an old man of him, although he was little over sixty; and he begged me to go with him. "I should like you to help me," he said. "I have a feeling that we might, perhaps, hear something about that young rascal of mine. 'Wounded and missing,' you know, always leaves one with just a hope."

The first beautiful release of peace was passing then into that restless craving for immense action which affected us all so strongly at that time; and the feeling was aggravated in my case by the realisation of impotence. I was too old to help.

I accepted Strickland's offer, eagerly....

I do not believe that he remembered his vision when, after a week's fruitless enquiry, we came one afternoon to the historic desert that had once been beautiful France. Certainly, he made no reference to his old experience; but he was almost senile. I noticed a difference in him, even in that one week.

But I remembered; and I had a fit of cold shivering that I could not control when we came out on to the awful plain that they now call The Plain of the Dead, and saw the figure of that one demented peasant, dressed in the grotesque relics of two nations' uniforms.

He was digging feverishly with his pointed spade, and I heard the ring of it as it struck.

It was not a turnip that he wrenched up.

The thing rolled towards us....

Young Strickland's head had always been a queer shape.

A DIFFERENCE OF TEMPERAMENT

The differences between "young" Royce and "old" Bunnett had a dramatic quality that stirred even the wearied indifference of Stamp and Co.'s counting-house to simple efforts in psychological analysis.

Young Royce was dark, square, and determined; a reasoned boaster, who verified his boasts by action. When he made what sounded like a very rash assertion, it was bad policy to contradict, and quite fatal to bet against him.

Old Bunnett was tall and thin, fair, drooping, and despondent. He seldom committed himself to a confident statement of opinion, but gravely, almost voluptuously, hoped for the worst on every possible occasion. He was, by the office's classification, of the same breed as "old Robinson," who had come into the firm as a boy of fourteen and had now served his employers faithfully for fifty-one years.

Royce found a delight in marking that likeness. "Bunny, my boy," he used to say, "you've come here to stop. When I come back here in twenty years' time I shall find you still at the same old grind. You'll never get out of it."

"Not so sure as I want to," was Bunny's single form of defence against this impeachment of his powers of initiative—that and a sniff. The sniff was his characteristic comment on life; a long and thoughtful substitute for speech. He was not more than ordinarily susceptible to colds in the head; and his sniff was less a physical function than a vehicle of mental expression.

Young Royce, however, wanted and meant to leave the firm "directly he could see his way," as he put it. He had a vein of prudence, or it may have been merely shrewdness, that was sometimes overlooked by those who had come a little to dread the threat of his boasting. The one consolation afforded to those who suffered under his implication of their feebleness was the reflection that he would almost certainly "go to the bad one of these days." Bunny, alone, was pessimist enough to admit that Royce would "get on." He had been known to add, "Sure to; he's the sort that gets on."

The office as a whole jealously disagreed with him; and in their vehement denouncement of Bunny's pessimism failed to recognise that underlying all the violent and obvious contrasts between Royce and Bunnett there was at least one point of likeness, inasmuch as they both believed in Royce. (The only likeness conceded by the office was the coincidence that both men were born in the same month of the same year, and had come into the firm of Stamp and Company on the same day.)

Royce had actually left the firm on the Saturday afternoon that first introduced him to Bunnett's mother on Hampstead Heath. He had "seen his way" as far as a job at Capetown—a very risky and uncertain affair, in the office's opinion.

He had a streak of romantic sentiment hidden away somewhere, and he had come up to the Spaniards' Road to "take a last look at London." He was leaning over the railings looking down across the Vale of Health, when he became aware of an arrested Bunnett sniffing profoundly at the back of a bath-chair.

"My mother," Bunnett said, by way of introduction, and then in a half-aside, "she's a bit of an invalid, but she's been a little better lately, ain't you, mother? This is the Mr. Royce I was telling you about. Just going out to South Africa."

Mrs. Bunnett pinched her mouth into a line of sympathetic disapproval. "It's a long way to go," she remarked—and sniffed thoughtfully.

She and her son were, Royce thought, as exactly alike as a couple of old sheep.

The job in Capetown proved even more uncertain than the office had hopefully predicted, and Royce presently migrated to Melbourne. Thence he drifted across to Hobart. A year later he had found a temporary post in Ceylon, then worked his way up the Bay of Bengal to Calcutta, and stayed there a month before he took ship to Tientsin. It was in 1909, seven years after he had left London, that he first put foot in America, landing at San Francisco, after crossing the Pacific from Yokohama by way of Hawaii.

In those seven years he had suffered and learnt many things, but if the staff of Stamp and Co.'s counting-house had met "young Royce" on his landing in California they would have found no difference in him. He came ashore with the boast that he meant to make money in America.

And, indeed, his apparent failure to win any financial success during those years of wandering was due rather to that streak of imaginative romance in him than to any weakness of character. It had been necessary for him to satisfy some lust for adventure and experience before he could settle down to achieve a worldly ambition. He knew himself well enough to recognise his own quality. He had a perfect confidence in his ability to make money eventually. And just as he had made good his boasts in the old days, so now he made good his determination to seek another form of romance in America.

It would be superfluous to trace the means of his ascent. He was so obviously the successful type that readily finds employment and opportunity in the United States. He had determination combined with initiative and imagination. It is doubtful if even the deliberate, conservative methods of Stamp and Co. could have overlooked his ability if he had elected to stay in the employ of that stately English concern.

He became an American citizen in 1913, but he did not revisit London until the autumn of 1917, when he came over on business as a representative of the Steel Trust. Arthur H. Royce had become a person of considerable importance and influence. He stayed at the Carlton Hotel during the progress of his negotiations with the English Government Department, the methods of which he ridiculed as being founded on the same principles as those familiar to him in the counting-house of Messrs. Stamp and Co.

But the old streak of romance showed itself again on the last Saturday of his stay in England. He had not called on the partners or employees of his old office. He had come to boast in action now, and the boast of language had become futile and unnecessary. He went up to the Spaniards' Road solely to satisfy some need for self-approval that he hoped to find in the contrast between his present condition and that in which he had last looked down over the hazy prospect of London, fifteen years before.

He was leaning over the rail in much the same place and attitude when he saw, with a strange thrill, the once familiar figure of old Bunnett coming towards him, pushing his invalid mother in what was surely the same bath-chair.

Royce straightened himself, and turned to meet them. He wondered if they would recognise him. There was something of the old self-conscious boast in his attitude as he held out his hand and said;

"Hullo! Bunny. Still here, then?"

Bunnett and his mother sniffed in concert, a deep and melancholy comment on life.

"Still here," agreed Bunnett, and his mother added, "So you're back in London, Mr. Royce?"

"For a few days," Royce admitted.

"South African job turn out all right?" Bunnett asked.

Royce hesitated. In one swift flash of retrospect he looked back on those full and varied adventures that had begun for him with the voyage to Capetown, and knew that though he stood there talking and boasting for a week, he could not convey to old Bunnett and his mother one-hundredth part of the romance and wonder that had glorified his existence for fifteen years.

"Oh! yes; all right," he said; "and you? Still with Stamps?"

And Bunnett, too, hesitated as if there were something he also lacked power to describe before he answered "Yes, still there."

The conversation seemed to offer no further possibilities. For a moment they stood awkwardly, and then Bunnett said, "My mother's a bit of an invalid, but she's been a little better lately." He sniffed thoughtfully.

As Royce made his way back to his hotel he modestly thanked God that he was not as some other men.

He had, however, missed one small observation. He had been standing on Bunnett's right side as they talked, and had not noticed that he had lost his left arm.

REFERENCE WANTED!

As usual, the compartment was nearly empty after we left Rickmansworth, and I anticipated that my one other fellow-passenger would probably get out at the next station and leave me to finish the dull journey alone. I did not, in any case, expect much entertainment from his society. He had a narrow forehead, and a preoccupied, rather scared, expression. It crossed my mind that he might have been a sufferer from shell-shock. I had seen that look in the eyes of one such case, a look at once timid, defensive, and suspicious. I was surprised when he came across the compartment to the seat opposite to me and began to talk.

We opened in the usual way by abusing the line, but he broke off in the middle to comment on the book I had been reading, Dostoievsky's The Possessed.

"Fine stuff, that," he commented, looked at me suspiciously for a moment, and then added, "What's that other book of his, Anna—something?"

"Anna Karenin?" I suggested.

He nodded.

"But that's Tolstoi," I said.

"Very likely," he replied; "I've no memory for some things. No memory at all. But I've read more than you might expect. To be quite honest, when I was a bit younger I read too much."

I pricked up my ears. I saw the promise of getting him to talk about himself. And I can listen to anything a man has to tell me of his own history; it is only men's opinions that I find so boring. Why will people have opinions?

"And overstrained your memory?" I asked.

He shook his head and pursed his mouth. "It wasn't that that ruined my prospects," he said.

"No?" I commented, as provocatively as I could.

He leaned a little forward and frowned with an effect of thoughtful concentration as he said, "You see, in some ways I've got too good a memory; the trouble with me is that I can't remember what I've remembered."

I raised my eyebrows interrogatively. I could see that he was warm, now, with the craving to confess himself.

"You aren't a writer, yourself, by any chance?" he asked.

"I've done a certain amount," I admitted.

"Thought you had rather that look," he said; and went on quickly as if he were afraid that I might, in the circumstances, be tempted to detail my own achievements; "and that being so, my case might interest you, professionally, as you might say."

"It certainly would, if you care to...." I began, but I saw that he was not listening. Those queer-looking eyes of his had taken on the expression of one who is engaged in some immense effort of memory.

"As a young man," he said—I guessed him to be, then, about thirty-five—"I had a great ambition to become a writer; but although my mind was full of ideas, I had no gift for putting them into language. At first, I tried in the ordinary way, just as all beginners do, to write stories for the magazines; but they none of them got accepted. Which wasn't to be wondered at. I knew myself how bad they were, and I used to console myself a little with that knowledge. I may have read somewhere that so long as you kept a cool head about your own writing, there was hope for you.

"Anyway, I left off writing for a time—I wasn't twenty then—and took to studying. I read all the best authors—carefully, trying to see how the thing was done. I had a lot of spare time one way and another, and in the next five years I got through a wonderful lot of reading. I didn't confine myself to English authors, either; I read a heap of translations from Russian, French, and German. And all that time I never once tried to write again, myself. I was just getting to learn my trade, I thought.

"Then I lost my job in the city, and while I was looking about for another one I had another shot at writing a magazine story. Well, it was certainly the nearest I'd got up to then of being the right thing. It was a lot better written than any of my other shots, but the plot was too weak. And I found that in learning to write I had lost all my ideas. I'd forgotten all the old ones, and no new ones came to me. At least, not at first."

He paused a moment and looked out of the window before he continued, rather abruptly: "An idea came to me, though, in the train one day—the best I'd ever had. And I not only saw the whole story clear in my mind, but I saw just how it ought to be written. I went home and began it at once. I had it finished in two days. A little masterpiece I thought it was. I submitted it to one of the reviews, and it was accepted within a week.

"A fortnight later I'd written another. It was very different from the first—done in another mood, as you might say, and lighter altogether. But that one came, too, as an inspiration, and was accepted by one of the magazines. And, after that, I used to get inspirations every other day almost—all sorts of inspirations. I saw myself as the most versatile and gifted writer of the day. I fancied that when my stories were collected and published in book form they would cause a lot of attention. By the time my second story appeared in the magazine—that was the first to get into print—I had written about eight altogether, and they'd all been taken by some editor or another—except one."

He paused again, and remained silent for so long that I prompted him by saying: "What was the matter with that one exception?"

He looked at me and sighed. "There wasn't anything wrong with the story, as you might say," he said; "but there was a note from the editor in which he said that my story appeared to be a translation from some French writer, I've forgotten the name, and should not have been submitted as an original contribution. Rather a nasty note it was.

"And about a week later my first story came out in the review, and then there was the devil to pay. It seems that that was a translation, too, from the Russian, and had been printed in English, in a collection of the fellow's works. His name began with a T, too, I fancy, but it wasn't Tolstoi."

"Turgenev?" I suggested.

"Very likely," he said wearily. "I can't remember. All I know is that every one of my stories were cribs. I'd remembered them all, and didn't remember that I'd remembered. Well, I got back all the stories that hadn't been published, but there was the very deuce of a row."

The train was drawing into Aylesbury, and my companion got up and collected his things from the rack. Before he got out, however, he paused to say, "Well, there you are. It was a dreadful experience for me, but if you can make any use of it, professionally, so to speak, you're welcome to it. Good-day to you."

I had still four more stations to go, and I sat on, turning over that strange confession in my mind. The man had appeared to be honest, the story sounded true as he told it, yet his phraseology and his accent were not those I should have expected from one of his literary experience.

But what worries me most of all is the vague but horribly persistent impression that somewhere, at some time, I have seen that story of his in print....

It is more than twenty years, now, since the late George Wallace came into the offices of Hallows and Rice one afternoon and talked to me about the novel he was writing. He was well known, even then, as journalist, essayist, playwright, and poet, and I welcomed with enthusiasm the suggestion that the firm of publishers for which I was then reader should consider the book when it was written. He told me in the strictest confidence that the title was to be As the Crow Flies, and gave me a hint of the subject he proposed to treat. Both title and subject were, I thought, admirable from every point of view, but he said that he would prefer me to say nothing to the firm about the novel until it was actually written. "Wait until you've read it, my dear chap," he said. "I haven't told another soul as yet, and I don't want to, until the thing's done and off my hands."

I did not see him again for nearly six months. He was the guest of the evening at a small literary dining club on that occasion, and when I went over and sat down by him, after the speeches, he instantly referred to our last interview by saying, "It's getting on, but we can't talk about it here. How's the business?" I told him that the business, so far as I was concerned, remained in a state of tense expectation for a really firstclass novel. He nodded with an air of satisfaction. "You shall have it," he said. "If you'll walk part of the way home with me I'll tell you something about it." He lived at Highgate, and my rooms were at Herne Hill, but I was prepared to miss the last train rather than lose that confidence. I was very eager in those days.

And I certainly did not regret the walk to Highgate and back, nor the two hours' wait at Ludgate Hill for the 3.15 "paper" train. Wallace let himself go that night, and made me realise that his novel was to be the best thing for years. He told me all about it. The book was to be a complete exposition of the British national character, as portrayed in the person of his hero, Joseph Blake. Blake was to be a success; a typical member of the middle class, educated at a grammar school, entering a business career at eighteen, and Parliament at forty-five; achieving cabinet rank at fifty-four, and the Premiership at sixty-three. As a background to the central figure there were to be any number of minor characters, all, as it were, supporting and representing Blake—"the firm mass of British opinion" Wallace called it. The single exception was to be a school friend of Blake's, a man of brilliant parts, but without social or personal ambitions, who spent his life in writing works of philosophy that nobody wanted to read. He was not poor, nor, in a sense, neglected—"we'll get away altogether from the typical romance," Wallace commented—but his work and life counted for nothing in popular opinion. The real climax of the book, and incidentally the very first suggestion that Blake was not a great man nor his friend ("I have thought of calling him John Rooke," Wallace said) a failure, was reached in the last few pages, when Blake, after a prolonged illness, and patiently waiting for death, confides in Rooke that he knows, now, that such a career as his had been was wasted effort. To which Rooke replies that he had known that at school.

"How much of the book have you written?" I asked Wallace just before we parted.

"About 80,000 words," he told me, "but I am not absolutely satisfied with some of the detail. What I propose to do is to finish the thing and then partly rewrite it."

He went to America on a long lecture-tour that autumn, and I did not see him again for twelve months. I sought him out, then, because McGillett made a casual reference to the magnum opus at lunch one day, and I realised that I was no longer the only recipient of Wallace's confidence. In those days one of McGillett's sources of income was finding books for publishers, and afterwards using what influence he had to get his discoveries well noticed in the Press; and when I found that he knew about the book, I was afraid that I might not, after all, get it for Hallows and Rice.

Wallace reassured me, however. He said that he never went back on a bargain, and when I pointed out to him that no bargain had been made as yet, he promised to call at the office next day and discuss terms with the partners. On my recommendation, the terms offered were amazingly liberal for a first novel; but my enthusiasm was powerful enough for once to overcome the awful inertia of old Hallows. (He had been in the publishing business for thirty years, and his one idea was to buy as cheaply as he could. He had no conception of what Rice and myself understood by "enterprise.") The firm even went so far as to offer to pay a proportion of the "advance" on signing the agreement, but Wallace refused to accept that. He said that it would harass him to feel tied; and he would not promise any particular date for the delivery of the manuscript. "I've nearly finished the book," he told us, "but when it's written, I want to put it away for three months and then go right through it again with a fresh mind. I mean this book to be a classic." Old Hallows was tremendously impressed, I remember, and congratulated me on having made "a real find."

After that agreement was signed I no longer felt it necessary to hold my tongue about the book, and I dropped a hint or two here and there as to what might be expected when it was published. I cannot believe, however, that I was the chief instigator of the steadily growing interest that was being aroused by the promise of Wallace's novel. No doubt both old Hallows and Rice made occasional references in public to the same subject, but I fancy that Wallace himself was the really active propagandist. In any case, one was continually finding references to As the Crow Flies in the Press that spring, even the name of Joseph Blake was sometimes referred to as an exemplar of the British character. The book was asked for at the libraries, and I more than once met people who declared that they had read it. At the office we had decided to print a first edition of 20,000 copies, and we put a note about it in our autumn list. Wallace assured me that summer (1899) that the thing was done and only needed a final revision. "If I died tomorrow," he said, "the story is all there ready to be published, but there is an incident or two that I want to alter before I send it along to you. I mean to deliver you a perfect manuscript. I sha'n't touch the thing in proof."

And then, of course, we did not press him for delivery in the autumn of that year. We should not, in any case, have published so important a book during the first months of the Boer war. And in the following spring Wallace himself went out to South Africa. I did not see him before he went. In fact, I did not know he had enlisted until I saw a reference to the fact in the "literary notes" that were just beginning to break out again in the daily and weekly papers.

In that paragraph Wallace's name was, as usual, coupled with that of his novel As the Crow Flies, a precedent that was invariably followed two months later in his obituary notices. (It will be remembered that he died of enteric in June 1900.) Many of the writers assumed that the book had already been published, but some of the better informed expressed their eagerness to read the book which they understood had been completed before Wallace went out to the front.

I firmly believe that our failure to discover that precious manuscript of Wallace's was the cause of old Hallows's breakdown and subsequent retirement from the business. He used to go up to Highgate two or three days a week to search Wallace's house for possible hiding places. "He would have been sure to have put it in some very safe place before he left the country," he would say, and then fret himself into a fever lamenting the "rank imbecility" of not having insisted on taking charge of the precious script before Wallace went away.

Rice's theory was that Wallace had taken the MS. with him to make his final revision, but I have often wondered whether Wallace had ever begun it. I have found a suggestion of that one fatal omission, in his title. He took too direct a method. So far as he was concerned, the book was written, and published, and noticed, without his having put pen to paper.

But the queer thing is that the unwritten book has outlived him. For some reason it was not forgotten in the stress of the South African war. And it will be remembered that, in the reaction of the first years of this century, As the Crow Flies was constantly "quoted," and that there was quite a controversy as to whether the figure of Joseph Blake did not stand for that of Joseph Chamberlain.

Indeed, I was tempted to put down these notes of the true facts of the case because a friend asked me yesterday where he could get a book called As the Crow Flies, by George Wallace. A man had told him, he said, that it was the finest novel of the century.

THE NIGHT OF CREATION

PART 1: THE DISCUSSION

I

The discussion had threatened while they were still at dinner. Leslie Vernon had begun it: and there had been a hardness and a determination in his expression that had sharpened the suggestion of fanaticism in his clever face. Little Harrison, already looking a trifle flushed and dishevelled, had only managed to avoid the direct issue by talking rapidly, and with something more than his usual brilliance, about the true inwardness of the Russian Revolution; a subject upon which he had recently acquired some very special information. Even Lady Ulrica More, who was manifestly prepared to encourage Vernon, had been borne down and fairly talked into silence.

The other guests of the week-end party, although they had shown no signs of disapproving Vernon's choice of topic when he had irrelevantly introduced it, had accepted their cue with a tactful readiness. Little Harrison was their host, and if he wished, as he obviously did, to avoid this topic of Psychical Research, it was their duty to support him. Moreover, Mrs. Harrison had cut in almost at once, with that bird-like flustered air of hers, to the effect that spiritualism was almost "worse than religion with some people" and never led to anything but recriminations. Vernon had smiled with a fine effect of self-control when she had said that, but before he could defend himself, Harrison at the other end of the table had got under way with an anecdote of Lenin's pre-revolution career in Switzerland.

And directly dinner was finished, he had suggested that they should take their coffee and liqueurs on the lawn under the cedar. There was excuse enough—it was a wonderful night—but Greatorex, the leader-writer, who had acquired a habit of always looking for secret motives, was probably right in calling the move to the garden "a clever dodge."

"Dodge?" enquired young Fell listlessly. He had sat through dinner with a melancholy air of wondering how people could be interested in spirits whether of the dead or of the Russians; but Greatorex had been too much engrossed in drawing his own inferences to take any notice of Fell's distraction.

"Rather," he said, taking Fell's arm. "Gives Harrison the chance of slipping off when he can't stand it any longer. In a room, it's a bit pointed to get up and go away, but out here Vernon'll probably find himself addressing Harrison's empty chair."

Fell sighed. "What's he want—Vernon, I mean?" he asked indifferently.

Greatorex was willing enough to explain. "He wants to bring Harrison to book," he said, leading his companion down towards the sunk fence out of earshot of the rest of the party. "You see, Vernon has been tremendously interested in that book of Schrenck-Notsing's. You've seen it, I expect? It's all about materialisations. Extraordinary stuff. They did get amazing results. The book's full of photographs of the materialisations. Licked Crookes's Katie King into a cocked hat. Well, Vernon's been writing about it all over the place. Says it proves that there is a form of matter unknown to science, and that until the sceptics have disproved that, they had better shut up about the problem of immortality and so on. And then Harrison came out with a leader in the Supplement, pooh-poohing the whole affair. Clever stuff, of course, but not very sound on the logical side."

"And Vernon wants to pin him down, I suppose?" Fell commented tepidly.

"He wants to have a straight argument," Greatorex said, and then sinking his voice to a confidential note, he continued, "And if you ask me, Fell, Harrison's afraid of spiritualism. I've seen him tackled before, and he loses his temper. He doesn't want to listen! You know the look that comes into a fellow's face when he's shutting his mind against you—a sort of resolution and concentration as if he'd got his eye on his own ideal somewhere in the middle distance, and did not mean to look away from it...." He paused in the very heart of his account of Harrison's perversity, suddenly struck by the application of his description to the present expression on Fell's face. "Pretty much the look you're wearing now, in fact," he concluded drily. "Sorry if I've been boring you."

Fell came back to a realisation of his lapse with a slight start. "No, no, rather not, Greatorex," he said. "I mean it wasn't that; the truth is I'm rather worried. I was thinking...." He waved his hand vaguely in the direction of the sunset, and added, "That, somehow, made me feel as if...."

Greatorex thrust his hands into the pockets of his dinner-jacket and turned round to observe the phenomenon that had distracted Fell's attention. For a moment his prominent nose and rather small head came out as an emphatic silhouette against the afterglow in the North-West; and to Fell, already deep in the languors of sentiment, presented an air of picturesque romance.

Since Fell had come out from the high-lights and conventional influences of the house, his determination had begun to give way. In the atmosphere of the dining-room, he had felt certain that he would be right in doing what he had come down here expressly to do. Phyllis was no wife for a Civil Servant in his position. He had seen the consequences of such marriages in the Service. They kept a man back. If he married her, he would lose just that extra fillip of influence which would make the difference between special appointments and the common routine of promotion that would leave him no better prospect than an ultimate income of at best ten or twelve hundred pounds a year. One could not expect Lady Ulrica, for example, to continue the patronage she seemed, at present, so willing to lend him, if he made a marriage of that kind. He had seen it all so clearly while they were at dinner, and although his heart had failed him at the thought of his coming interview with Phyllis—she was so sweet and so gentle and she loved him with such an amazing singleness and rapture—he had been sure that he must give her up before his honour was entangled.

But now all the prestige of social success, everything that was represented by the fashion he had just left, was dwindling and fading; the effect of it falling away so that it seemed to him garish and unreal—as the lights and distractions of the town may seem to a man who sets his face eagerly towards the joy of his quiet home. The rest and immensity of nature was an enduring reality with which his love was in perfect accord. He and Phyllis had their place in it. If he could step down, now, to the sombre yews at the lake's edge and take her in his arms, as he had done a month ago, his last doubts would vanish on the instant. They would be one with the greatness of earth, and able to look down with contempt from their perfect enthronement, at the frivolous and ephemeral superficiality of conventional life....

The sound of Greatorex's voice seemed to take up the thread of his dreams.

"'Course, you're a poet, Fell," Greatorex said. "You feel an evening like this, I suppose? Means something quite tremendous to you?"

"You see," Fell began, trembling on the verge of confession; "there is a reason why, more particularly, to-night...."

Greatorex turned round and looked at him. "I shouldn't," he said. "You'll be sorry afterwards. Better not tell me. I know I look romantic, but I'm not. Harrison says I ought to have been a pirate. He's wrong, I ought to have been a barrister. I'll tell you, now, just what I've been thinking while I've been looking at all this view that makes you feel so sentimental. I've been thinking that I wouldn't like to have a lake so near the house—unhealthy. And I don't care for all those black yews, either. Melancholy, mournful, things."

Fell shuddered. "They are mournful," he agreed, "but they're in keeping."

"Too much," Greatorex said. "I don't know whether it's your sentimental influence or not, Fell; but, damn it, this place makes me feel superstitious, to-night. It's so infernally quiet and brooding, as if it were hatching some nasty mischief."

"Or some wonderful miracle?" Fell suggested.

"We probably mean the same thing," Greatorex said. "I've got a trick of using prose words to get attention. 'Wonderful miracle,' you know, would be either a cliché or bombast in a leader."

Fell did not appear to hear this explanation. He was looking out over the swell of Orton Park that was separated from Harrison's garden by the width of the lake. The afterglow was slowly dying and the greens of turf and wood were deepening and hardening into dark masses little softer than the funereal shadows of the clustered yews. The detail that had recently started into almost excessive prominence under the level light of the setting sun, was taking refuge in the temporary darkness before it emerged again altered in shape and colour to greet the mysteries of the moon. Only the lake still shone faintly, reflecting a last glimmer of brightness in the Northern sky. Near the island, a streamer of indigo ripples splayed out to mark the course of some belated water-bird, hurrying back to the cover of the reeds; and in the hush of the coming night Fell could almost believe that he heard the delicate clash and whisper of infinitely tiny waves breaking in hasty processional upon the sandy foreshore.

"'Straordinarily peaceful," murmured Greatorex. "Suppose we ought to be joining the others?"

"Yes, I suppose we ought," Fell agreed tamely. What else was there to do? He could not go down to the village of Long Orton now, and beseech Phyllis to come out and walk with him by the lake. And without her, all the glory of this amazing night was wasted.

Nor was the full promise of the night yet revealed to him; for it was not until with a reluctant sigh he had turned to follow Greatorex back to the nearly invisible group under the cedar, that he saw the Hunter's moon, a great disc of ruddy copper, resting as it seemed on the very edge of the eastern horizon.

He lingered, gazing, for a few seconds, half resolved even now to escape the banalities of polite conversation on the lawn and go up to the village. This was such a rare night for the silences of love; serene, brooding and mystical. Yet the automaton in him, the formalised, cultured habit of the Civil Servant, moved him relentlessly back towards the decencies of polite society and the patronage of Lady Ulrica More.

As he silently approached the group on the lawn he heard the clear, musical voice of Leslie Vernon.

"At least you might let one state a case, Harrison," he was saying.

II

They had already passed the stage of skirmishing for position, when Greatorex rejoined them. Something had apparently happened to Harrison since he came out into the garden. He had lost that effect of impatience which had underlain all his talk of Russia, when, as though afraid of silence, he had been talking, a trifle desperately, against some latent opposition.

Now, comfortably relaxed in the depth of a well-designed basket chair, and little more of him visible than the gleam of his shirt front, the pale blur of his face and the occasional glow of his cigarette end, he had an air of being tolerantly complacent. It seemed that he was willing to listen, however condescendingly, to Vernon's attack.

"Look here, Harrison," Vernon had begun. "Why won't you talk this out?"

"Nothing fresh to say," Harrison had replied.

"But I have," Vernon continued; and then Lady Ulrica definitely put her weight into the scale by saying, "How fascinating! Something really new in the way of evidence?"

"Or only a réchauffé?" Harrison interpolated.

"At least you might let one state a case," Vernon said as Greatorex joined the other four and sat down with a grunt beside his wife.

"We saw you gesticulating picturesquely against the sunset, G.," Harrison remarked, as though he would even now create a diversion and defer the discussion indefinitely.

Greatorex snorted; quite conscious of the fact that in Harrison's presence he always played up in manner to that part of the buccaneer which had been thrust upon him, although he disclaimed it in speech.

"Been discussing the effects of sunset on temperament," he said.

"But did you see the Moon?" asked Mrs. Harrison, rather in the tone of one who introduces a delightful piece of scandal.

"Afraid I missed that," Greatorex said. "But I expect Fell has found it. He's probably worshipping now."

"Oh! but you ought," Mrs. Harrison asserted, still intent no doubt, on keeping away from the subject of spiritualism, for her husband's sake. "It was like a rather badly done stage moon balanced on the scenery. Sha'n't we all go and worship with Mr. Fell?"

No one moved, however; and the excuse of joining Fell was spoilt by his arrival at the cedar.

"Do help yourself to coffee and anything you want, Mr. Fell," Mrs. Harrison said. "If you can see, that is." She was certainly doing her best to keep the conversation at the right after-dinner level. She was so far successful that for a minute or two little spurts of irrelevant talk continued to start up and die away again, like the uncertain catspaws of wind before a flat calm.

It was Harrison himself who at last anticipated the inevitable. He must have felt, as everyone had— including his plucky but finally despairing wife—that it was inevitable. There was something that urged them, something more than that quiet determination of Vernon's, although his very silence conveyed a perpetual sense of remonstrance. But this other, greater influence was with them as an almost palpable presence. It was like a force exhausting them and drawing them into a common focus.

None of them was more keenly aware of it than Fell, though he attributed the weakness that was overcoming him to a particular source. For here, with the arm of his chair almost touching that of Lady Ulrica's, he was planning an interview with Phyllis that held no least hint of the renunciation of love. He was giving way freely and without reserve to his dream. Moreover, he had a curious sense of instant accomplishment, as if at that very moment his spirit and the spirit of Phyllis had touched and coalesced. He was drifting into far heights of remote and supernal ecstasy, when the thin, high voice of Harrison recalled him to earth; and he started as though, on the verge of sleep, he had been brutally jarred and awakened by the violent slamming of a door.

"Hm! hm! Well, Vernon," Harrison said. "We're all waiting for that statement of your case."

Vernon's chair creaked slightly as if he had suddenly leaned forward.

This moment of their beginning, when by some undivinable act of common consent all oppositions had been temporarily relinquished and they were agreed at least to listen, was, also, the moment of greatest darkness. Presently the moon transmuted from copper to brass would rise above the house and give validity and form to all that was now being created in the profundity of the night. But when Vernon began to speak, he was hidden from them; they realised him only as a voice, that issued with a steady and increasing definition out of the silence and the shadows.

He talked well, pleading without passion for an unprejudiced examination of all the new "facts" in psychical research. He had a scholarly knowledge of his subject and gave his instances and authorities, building up as it seemed to Lady Ulrica, to Fell, and even to Greatorex, a case that it would be very hard to knock down.

Not once did Harrison interrupt him, and during Vernon's occasional pauses the immense stillness of the night seemed to close in upon the little group under the cedar with a sudden intensity. The slender stream of his steady speech was like a little candle, burning delicately in the darkness, and when it was extinguished, his listeners were freshly aware of themselves and their surroundings. In those moments of almost painful silence, they sought to recover their consciousness of the familiar world by restless movements and faint articulations. Chairs creaked, someone sighed, and once Greatorex rather brutally coughed.

Nearly at the end of his long speech, however, Vernon's tone became more emotional. He was talking, then, of materialisations and of the strange and as yet unrecognised form of matter—provisionally known as the ectoplasm or teleplasm—that issues from the body of the medium, is manifested in visible forms that can be successfully photographed, and can handle material objects.

"I claim that the existence of this matter is proved," Vernon concluded. "Given favourable conditions, the medium can build up a form, visible, tangible, ponderable and capable of simulating every appearance of material reality. I don't say that this amazing phenomenon proves the immortality of the soul, but I do say that until you produce another hypothesis to cover the immense accumulation of tested facts, you have no right to pronounce any opinion in psychical research."

By this time the moon, now pale as scoured brass, had topped the trees behind the house, and was sending out pale and slender shafts of light to pierce here and there the overshadowing gloom of the wide cedar: one shaft had dappled the statuesque bare shoulder of Lady Ulrica, and another had slanted down upon the smooth fair hair of Leslie Vernon. And by such reflections and by other sources of faint diffusion, the heavy brooding darkness that had so far enveloped the group on the lawn, had been definitely lifted. Dimly they could see each other, either as shadows against the increasing brightness beyond, or as weakly illuminated figures picked out, maybe, by a brilliant little spark of moonshine that had pierced its way through some common opening in the many-storied foliage above.

And although there had come no least stir of wind to break the intense calm, the releasing effect of the light was manifest upon the spirits of the party. As Vernon ceased speaking everyone suddenly wanted to talk. A little fusillade of chatter broke out, which only gave way when Greatorex was heard saying: "If he believe not Stainton Moses and the Lodges, neither will he believe though one rose from the dead."

Mrs. Harrison laughed brightly. "We must remember that," she said.

"But it's not a question of rising from the dead at all, Mr. Greatorex," Lady Ulrica put in. She had no sense of humour.

Vernon apparently felt that all the effect of his long argument was being foolishly dissipated by this absurd interruption. "Well, Harrison, what's your answer to my case?" he asked in a slightly raised voice.

Harrison began to stammer, a sure sign that his temper was at last beginning to conquer him. "I—I can't see, even if we admit the validity of these materialisations," he said, "that you—you are any nearer to proving your general case, Vernon. I've been into the whole question very thoroughly and—and impartially, and I can only say that I see no reason whatever to assume that we have ever received any communication from the spirits of the dead. I think that that is the real point under discussion, and I can't see that you've done much to support your contention. What d'you say, G.?"

Greatorex grunted. A beam of moonlight had just caught the most salient of his features, and at the moment his face appeared to be all nose.

"You won't accept my explanation of the facts, Harrison?" Vernon persisted.

"I—I don't see why I should," Harrison replied. "I don't see the necessity for it. I—I'm not convinced, by any means, of the validity of your examples. At present, I am content to go on with the enquiry without formulating any theory. I contend that the evidence up to the present time is insufficient to theorise upon."

"Ah! well, there's a lot more coming," Vernon replied, and for the first time a real note of passion crept into his voice. "Don't you realise that all these developments taken together are just the first stages of the knowledge that is coming to us? They are symptoms, that's all, of the new trend in the evolution of mankind; of the coming of the new age—the age of the Spirit. The days of materialism are nearly spent, and the next generation will smile at our feeble tentatives.

"Do you ask me how I know? Well, I can't tell you in terms that you can understand. The best part of my knowledge is intuitional, but intuition, even mysticism, must no longer be divorced from science and intellect. That, I feel, is the essential synthesis of the new doctrine. We are going to produce our material proofs; in the future religion and science will become one."

"My own opinion, precisely," said Lady Ulrica.

But Vernon's homily had proved a little too much for Harrison. He tried to speak and could not control the pitch of his voice, which soared ineffectively to a falsetto squeak.

"Er—er—I—I ..." he began, and had to get to his feet before he could attain coherence. Then he started again with "No, no! It's incredible nonsense that—the kind of religion foreshadowed by spiritualism—could ever appeal to sensible men and women. Are we to be expected to listen to the drivelling platitudes of some supposed spirit communicating through an illiterate old woman with the further interposition of a 'control,' speaking pigeon English and imitating the worst sophistications of a spoilt child? No, no, positively I can't take that kind of nonsense seriously. I—I have no sort of desire to imitate the credulity of Lodge, Barrett and Crookes—no sort of desire. I—I—it's absurd. I've no patience even to talk about it. Who is coming to look at the moon?" And without waiting to receive any response to his invitation, he turned his back on the cedar and strode out, a perturbed and impatient little figure, into the light of the open garden.

The other six followed him in a straggling procession.

Emma Harrison was obviously relieved that the discussion was at an end. "I said it would only end in recriminations," she explained to Greatorex, who looked about seven feet high in contrast with her diminutive slenderness. "Charles never can keep his temper about that subject. And I did think it was very splendid of him to keep it as long as he did. We can't do with all that nonsense. Can you, Mr. Greatorex?"

Mrs. Harrison dropped her voice to an indiscreet confidence. "I always think that our poor dear Lady Ulrica," she whispered, "is so very much the type from which mediums are made. You know, stout, placid, and not too clever."

"Queer thing why mediums should generally be so stupid," commented Greatorex, tactfully avoiding any overt agreement with his hostess's description of Lady Ulrica.

For a few minutes the party drifted about the lawn in couples, with the exception of Harrison, who maintaining a little distance from the others was pacing restlessly up and down, either working off his spleen or thinking out some really telling retort that should settle Vernon's business once and for all.

The moon was now high in the heavens, but it had suffered another transmutation. A faint screen of misty cirrus had crept over the sky, and the brass was toned down almost to the whiteness of silver. And with this change, the light in the garden had become more diffused. The shadows had lost their hardness, the high-lights their accentuation.

And by degrees, some sense of a peculiar quality in the night began to affect every member of the little party on the lawn. They began by almost imperceptible changes in their movements to drift together into a little knot, like the swimming bubbles in a cup. The area of their promenade diminished until even Harrison himself had come into the focus; and yet when they had again drawn into a group they had nothing to say to one another. It is true that they were still conscious of a slight social constraint, due to what had amounted to a quarrel between the host and one of his guests. But there was something in their attitude and their common movement towards each other that suggested some deeper cause for their momentary awkwardness. It was as if each of them was aware of some sudden fear, and hesitated to speak lest the shameful fact should be revealed.

It was Mrs. Harrison who first broke a silence that was becoming altogether too insistent—even the soft hush of their feet upon the grass had ceased. She laughed artificially, with a touch as it seemed of bravado, a laugh that might have disguised a shudder.

"I don't know how it seems to you," she said in a high strained voice, "but it strikes me that it's actually getting a little chilly."

"Yes, yes. It is, Emma," her husband replied with an effect of relief. "I—I think we'd better go in. We get a cold air off the lake, now and again," he explained to the company at large.

"Precious little air, Harrison," muttered Greatorex. "I've never known a stiller night."

"Haze come over the moon," commented Fell, staring up into the sky.

"It has certainly turned colder," remarked Lady Ulrica with a shiver; "much colder."

Harrison cleared his throat and made his usual effort to get his pitch. "Hm! Hm! Perhaps we're going to get some phenomena," he said with a slightly cracked laugh. "Always the first warning, isn't it, Vernon, a draught of cold air?"

"Always," Lady Ulrica said solemnly, before Vernon could reply.

Harrison was about to speak again when Greatorex cut in. "I say," he said, in a voice that held a just perceptible note of excitement, "is that one of your maids down there by the lake? Girl in white; moving about by the yews?"

"What do you mean?" Mrs. Harrison replied, speaking with a little flurry of haste. "It must be after eleven, and the maids are in bed long ago, I hope."

"Someone down there, anyway," Greatorex asserted.

"Hm, hm! G.'s quite right, my dear," Harrison said. "I—I think we ought to investigate this in the cause of common morality."

"Charles? It may be one of the village girls," his wife suggested.

"In which case she has no business in our paddock at midnight," Harrison replied, and as he spoke he began to walk with an air of mechanical determination towards the steps in the sunk fence that led to the meadow.

"Shall we all go?" Greatorex asked, but Mrs. Harrison manifestly hesitated.

"I don't know. Do you think, perhaps...." she began.

Greatorex, however, had not waited for her permission, and in half a dozen strides he too had reached the meadow. Vernon, Lady Ulrica and Mrs. Greatorex followed him with an effect of yielding to a sudden impulse, and Emma found herself alone on the lawn with Robert Fell.

"Well, if they're all going," she said with a little hysterical laugh, "I suppose we may as well go, too."

"I don't know. Yes. Do you think we ought?" Fell replied in a strangely agitated voice.

Mrs. Harrison turned to look at him with a little start of surprise. "Surely you're not afraid?" she asked, unconsciously revealing the cause of her own reluctance.

"Afraid?" he echoed, entirely misunderstanding her true intention. "Afraid of what?"

"Well—ghosts!" she said.

"But you don't really imagine, Mrs. Harrison...." Fell began.

"Not for one moment," she said with determination. She was disturbed and a trifle shocked by the marks of his agitation, which had nevertheless stiffened her own courage. She was prepared now to demonstrate how little she cared for an unexpected coldness in the air, or for white figures moving about at the most unlikely hours on the borders of the lake.

Already the shadows of the other five were stringing out across the meadow, all of them clearly visible in the milky light of the thinly veiled moon. They were moving very deliberately; but a certain deliberation of approach was only decent if they expected to disturb a tryst.

"Well, aren't you coming, Mr. Fell?" Emma asked sharply.

He sighed and then, "Yes, I'll come," he said, in the tone of one who finally commits himself.

PART 2: THE APPEARANCE

I

Harrison and Fell were within a few yards of the plantation, when the vague pillar of illusive whiteness that flitted in the shadow of the trees moved towards them, and, after the slight hesitation of one who dreads to plunge, stepped into the moonlight. But having thus dared the shock of immersion, it seemed that for the moment her strength could carry her no further. She stood motionless and with an effect of strained effort, on the shadow, her eyes downcast and her crossed hands grasping the ends of the tulle scarf that draped her head and shoulders.

In that stiff pose, with the rigid lines of her figure delivered milk-white against the sullen background of the yews, she looked less like a human being than the rather conventional image of some idealised virgin, the expression of a dream, modelled none too definitely in wax by an artist whose recollection of his vision was already fading.

Harrison stopped short and laid his hand on Fell's arm. "Who is it?" he asked him. It was manifestly an absurd question to put to his companion, a stranger in Long Orton; but in the first agitation of the discovery Harrison clutched at the nearest support.

"No idea!" Fell replied. He was suddenly disappointed and downcast. This girl, whoever she might be, was certainly not Phyllis, and all the furious expectations and fine resolves that had wonderfully lighted him had been quenched with an abruptness that left him listless and momentarily devoid of curiosity.

"Who is it?" repeated Greatorex, who had been only a pace or two behind them. He spoke in the tone a man might use while surreptitiously addressing his neighbour during a church-service. This echo of his own question seemed to annoy Harrison. He shrugged his shoulders contemptuously, and turning round addressed his wife in a voice that was unnecessarily strident.

"Here's a mysterious lady come to call upon us, Emma," he said.

And then Mrs. Harrison, giggling nervously, put the essential but manifestly hopeless question for the third time.

"Who is she?" she asked, in an undertone.

Harrison may have hoped that the shock of his voice, and, perhaps, of his determinedly sceptical attitude, would have exorcised the phantom that was assuredly, so he had already decided, the creation of a moment's excited imagination. But when he turned back to face the plantation, the pale figure still stood in the same attitude, and seemed now, moreover, to have attained a sharper definition of outline; to be altogether more human and solid.

"By Jove, you know, it is someone, after all," Harrison murmured.

"Oh! it is someone, right enough," Fell said, at present concerned only with the fact that it was not the right someone.

"Oh! Well!" Harrison softly ejaculated, as one who braces himself to an encounter.

He stepped forward a couple of paces with a slightly grotesque air of greeting. "Hm! hm! I don't quite know ..." he said; "that is, might I ask whom we have the pleasure of—of meeting so unexpectedly?"

The frozen intensity of the silence that appeared to follow his question may have been due to the fact that each member of the party was holding his or her breath in the expectation of the moment.

The figure moved. Slowly and with an almost painful deliberation she released the ends of the tulle scarf that was about her head and shoulders, and let her hands fall to her sides. Her mouth opened, but she did not speak; and after what might have been another effort to reply—a just perceptible movement of the head—she took a careful step backward, entering again the shadow of the yews.

"But, I say, you know...." Harrison began.

She interrupted him with a gesture, raising her hand and pointing with an unmistakable certainty at Lady Ulrica. And the hand and forearm that by this gesture she once more plunged into the moonlight had something the appearance of opalescent glass.

Harrison, standing with his back to the house-party, did not understand this indication and turned his head to see who or what had been selected for peculiar notice; but Lady Ulrica responded with a fine dignity. She came forward past Harrison right up to the edge of the yews, and said in a voice that did credit to her breeding:

"My dear, what is it? Can I help you in any way?"

And then, no doubt to the infinite relief of the Harrisons, the unknown replied. She had a little husky voice when she first spoke, a voice that suggested the last sleepy clutter of roosting birds; and her speech came with an appearance of effort.

"Presently," she said rather indistinctly, and added something that sounded like "more strength."

Lady Ulrica was painfully short-sighted. She had those large, protuberant brown eyes, almost devoid of expression, that are sometimes indicative of heart trouble. And as she answered, she was fumbling at her breast for the impressive, handled lorgnette that was discovered later on the coffee table under the cedar.

"We weren't quite sure, you know," she said in her authoritative contralto; "whether you were an apparition or not, and so we came to see. But, of course, now we have seen you and heard you speak, we shall be delighted to help you if you want help, or—if you'd prefer it—to go away."

"Stay near me," the stranger said in a clearer voice, and striking a lower pitch than when she had spoken first. "Till I get more strength."

The rest of the party had paused in a little knot, some six or seven feet away, while this brief conversation had gone forward, listening staring with an absorption that in other circumstances might have been judged as slightly lacking in good taste. But now, some kind of realisation of their attitude seemed to come to them, and they diverted their attention by a manifest effort from the two people on the edge of the plantation and began to talk in low voices among themselves.

Mrs. Harrison, moving across to her husband, looked at him with raised eyebrows, silently asking the obvious question.

"Fraud," he said in a careful undertone, and added rather more viciously, "Hoax of some kind."

Mrs. Harrison, however, was not to be rebuffed so easily. "But, Charles," she said with a slight urgency, as if she would persuade him to be reasonable; "don't you think there is something very odd about her? As if she were not quite sane? That pose of the Virgin Mary when she was in the moonlight as we came up? And did you notice that she's wearing quite the commonest sort of tulle scarf?"

"Yes, I'd noticed that," he began, and then their attention was snatched back to their strange visitor by the sound of a laugh. It was a clear, high laugh, but just too near the edge of emotion for a person under suspicion of madness.

"I must see to this," Harrison murmured to his wife, and took a few steps towards Lady Ulrica and the mysterious visitor. He was a connoisseur of feminine beauty, and he had been struck by what he mentally termed the "exquisite accuracy" of the profile presented to him. It had come clear and sharp against the background of the plantation, white and vivid in the moonlight; a forehead in a vertical line over the delicately rounded chin, a perfectly curved aquiline nose and the suggestion of a fine, sensitive mouth. Harrison saw it as the considered and patient modelling of some idealised profile in a cameo. It was a type that he very greatly admired; and this sight of her beauty perhaps softened the asperity of the cross-examination he had intended.

He came within a few feet of her as he began to speak, but she was still within the black shadow of the trees and he could no longer distinguish her features.

"We—we are rather at a loss, my dear young lady," he said. "You understand, I hope, that if you find yourself in any perplexity, my wife will be delighted to offer you our hospitality."

Instead of answering him she put out her hand towards Lady Ulrica, but when that lady made a responsive movement, the stranger shrank away again.

"They don't help me," she murmured. An undercurrent of agitation was coming into her speech, and began to dominate it as she continued, more hurriedly; "I can't help it, if they won't believe me. They're antag—antago—tell them to be still—in their thoughts—in their...."

Her voice died out, fluttering down through the original quality of huskiness that had first distinguished it, to a hoarse, diminishing whisper. And it seemed at the same moment as if she also were stealthily retreating, sliding away from them.

"Look out! She's going!" Harrison cried out. "We mustn't let her get away like this. She's—she's not safe to be left alone. We must catch her."

But already the stranger was nearly out of sight. For an instant they saw her through the darkness, as an illusive pillar of faint light gleaming among the profound shadows of the yews; a pale uncertain form that vanished even as they started in pursuit.

"I'm going to get to the bottom of this," Harrison announced with determination as he led the search.

Yet, from the very outset, that search was the most perfunctory and futile affair. The members of the party, two of whom stayed behind, exhibited a marked inclination not to separate. Outside, in the security of the moonlight and each other's society, they had suffered mystification, wonder, perhaps an occasional thrill of apprehension, but not that peculiar quality of fear that lay in wait for them the moment they entered the gloom of the plantation.

II

Even Greatorex felt that influence. He had followed his host, in advance of the other three, but lost sight of him directly as he entered the cover of the trees. He started violently when a twig brushed his face, and then, with a just perceptible note of alarm in his voice, called out:

"Hallo, Harrison! You there? It's so infernally dark!"

Harrison answered him with a remarkable promptitude.

"Hallo, G.!" he said. "That you? I'm close here! I'll wait for you."

They were as a matter of fact separated only by the spread of a single yew.

"Don't see that we stand much chance of catching the lady in a place like this, Harrison," Greatorex remarked when they had joined company. "You might hide a platoon under these trees in this light, what?"

"Only a narrow belt of it," Harrison replied. "We'll be through on to the shore of the lake in ten yards. We can see her then for half a mile if she's come out."

"All right," Greatorex agreed, and added in a mood of sudden confidence; "Beastly weird sort of place, this, but it's been a weird sort of affair altogether."

"Mad woman," commented Harrison with a touch of vehemence.

"Queer, certainly," Greatorex agreed. "But why did you say hoax, just now? You don't think that...?"

They had been talking in interrupted snatches as they pressed their way, keeping close together, through the stubborn resistance of the yews, but as Greatorex's sentence trailed away with a suggestion of cutting off his own suspicions, they came out on to the long grass that bordered the lake.

Harrison stopped, and gave a sigh that may have indicated his relief at getting clear from the intriguing opposition of the plantation.

Before them was spread the placid deep of the black water, so calm and rigid that it looked like a sheet of unsoiled and faintly lustrous ice. To the right and left of them the bank ran in a flat curve, in full sight for a quarter of a mile each way, save that it was bordered by an uneven selvage of impenetrable black shadow. But nowhere was there any sign of a flitting white shape, escaping from the charges of hoax or insanity that had been brought against it.

"Either got away or hiding in the plantation," remarked Greatorex, after a pause during which with a suggestion of breathless eagerness the two men had searched the moonlit distances. The wreath of cirrus had cleared away now, and the moon had reached the perfect gold of its ultimate splendour.

"Hm!" Harrison replied thoughtfully. "Not much good searching the plantation."

"Might as well hunt for a louse in a woodstack," Greatorex thought.

"What did you make of it, G.?" Harrison asked suddenly.

"Mighty queer business altogether," Greatorex replied. And then with a sudden drop in his voice, he added on a note of alarm, "What the devil is that you've got on your back, Harrison?"

"Eh? What? What d'you mean?" Harrison asked nervously.

Greatorex took a step towards him, and after a moment's pause in which he hesitated as if afraid to touch some uncanny thing, laid hold of a long wisp of drapery and stripped it from his host's back and shoulders. It seemed to Greatorex that the flimsy thing clung slightly to the smooth cloth of the dinner jacket.

"What is it? What is it?" asked Harrison impatiently.

"Looks like that scarf the apparition was wearing," Greatorex remarked, displaying it.

Harrison clutched at it eagerly.

"By Jove, so it is!" he said; "tangible proof, this, G., of the lady's substantiality. Good, solid evidence of fact. They must all have seen it. Emma even mentioned it to me as being of rather common material." As he spoke he was fingering the stuff of the scarf; running it through his hands, as if he found an almost sensual pleasure in the reassuring quality of its undoubted substance.

"Why, of course," Greatorex answered, little less relieved than his companion; but anxious, now, to prove that he had never for one instant been under any delusion as to the nature of the apparition. "You never thought, did you, that the lady was a ghost?" His laugh as he asked the question had a slightly insincere ring, but Harrison was too preoccupied with his own thoughts to notice that.

"A ghost! My dear G.!" he said. "The ghost of what, in Heaven's name? No, no, she was solid enough. But what's puzzling me is whether she was insane, or whether, as seems to me more probable, the whole thing was a hoax of some kind."

"You don't suggest that Vernon, or Lady Ulrica...." Greatorex began, but Harrison cut him short.

"No, certainly not," he said. "They would not be so silly. It was just a coincidence that we should have been discussing all this foolishness beforehand. No, there are thousands of deluded idiots about, of one sort or another, who have gone mad on this spiritualism business, and I think the most probable explanation is that some week-end visitor at the hotel—we've got quite a decent hotel in the village, you know, kept by a fellow called Messenger—some woman or other, a little cracked on this subject, came out here and was tempted to try a little experiment on us. Probably she didn't mean to go quite so far, in the first instance. Just showed herself in the moonlight, playing at being an apparition for our benefit. She'd be able to see us on the lawn from here. And then when we caught her, she had to play up to the part. No doubt, she recognised Lady Ulrica's credulity. Recognised her as the kind of woman that makes the fortune of the ordinary medium. And all that nonsensical talk of hers—not badly done, in a way, by the by—was just the sort of stuff they spew up at a séance. Eh? Don't you agree? What we've got to do now is to find out who it was. We'll go down and talk to Messenger tomorrow morning, and get the truth about it. He's got an uncommonly pretty daughter, by the way; and I don't think we'll take Fell. He showed signs of being a trifle épris in that quarter, when he was down here last."

Harrison's confidence grew as he spoke, and before he had finished he had warmed to quite a glow of certainty. His excitement had something the quality of that displayed by one who finds himself unhurt after a nasty accident.

"Expect you're right," Greatorex agreed calmly.

"Well, we'd better get back to the others—with our—our evidence." Harrison looked down at the scarf in his hands, and began automatically to fold it as he spoke. "There's a path through the plantation, a few yards further up," he continued. "No need for us to tear ourselves to pieces among the shrubs. As you said, we haven't the least chance of finding the lady by this light, and the only decent thing we can do is to clear off, and let her find her way back to the hotel."

"If your theory is the right one," Greatorex commented, as they began to walk up the bank of the lake.

"Have you a better?" snapped Harrison.

"No—no," Greatorex admitted. "Can't say I have. And anyway, yours is susceptible of proof. All we have to do is to find the lady."

"Quite so," Harrison said without conviction. He foresaw, with a little qualm of uneasiness, that his failure to produce the lady might prove a difficulty in any controversy that might follow with Vernon and Lady Ulrica. If he definitely committed himself to a theory that could be upheld or discredited by the investigation of verifiable facts, he would be at an immense disadvantage should the facts go against him—as, he was ready to admit to himself, they very possibly might. He realised that in his excitement he had been too hasty.

"Of course, G.," he said on a faintly expostulating note, "of course, I may have been rather premature in assuming that this—er—visitor of ours was staying at the hotel. I—I don't in any way insist on that. It's our first chance and perhaps our best one; but there are other alternatives. We can begin with this scarf. That's our solid ground of evidence. What we have to do is to trace the owner."

"Exactly," Greatorex agreed thoughtfully.

Harrison noticed the sound of a qualification in his friend's reply.

"Well, isn't it?" he asked.

"Yes, oh yes; that's all right," Greatorex agreed. "I was only wondering why, after all, we should bother any more about it?"

Harrison was too clever a man to attempt evasions. He saw quite clearly that if he pretended some more or less plausible excuse such as being annoyed by the trespass, Greatorex would see through him. And he would not risk that. Instead, he took what seemed a perfectly safe line.

"To be quite honest, G.," he said, "I am fully anticipating that Vernon will claim this—this experience, as being a spiritualistic phenomenon. And—and—well, I'll admit that that attitude annoys me. It's so childish. This seems to me a—a perfectly fair instance of the sort of thing that these credulous people take hold of and transform into what they call proof. Properly garbled, as no doubt it will be, this silly little incident will presently be figuring in the Proceedings of the S.P.R. as 'new evidence.' Vernon could dress it up to look as circumstantial as the evidence in a police-court—give all our names and addresses, and make out affidavits for us to sign—affidavits that would not contain a single mis-statement of fact so far as we can see, but taken altogether would have an entirely false significance. You know how the...." He broke off suddenly in the middle of his sentence. "What the devil's that?" he asked sharply.

He had paused in his walk, as was his habit when he wished to elaborate an argument, and they had not yet left the bank of the lake for the path through the plantation. What had so abruptly diverted his attention was the beginning of a sound in that airless night, a sound that, as they waited and listened, waxed from the first insistent whispering with which it had begun, to a fierce rustling that seemed to swell almost to a roar, before it died again to the hushed sibilance of the outset.

"What the devil is it?" Greatorex muttered.

Harrison gave a little scream of half-hysterical laughter.

"Our—our nerves must have been very thoroughly upset, G.," he said in a strained voice, "if—if you and I can be startled by the sound of wind in the poplars. They're on the island there, a big clump of them. Now I think of it, that's one of the things that made this place so confoundedly unfamiliar to-night. It's the first time I've ever been here when it has been so still that the poplars weren't talking."

"Wind!" ejaculated Greatorex. "There is no wind."

"There has been," Harrison said, and pointed to the lake whose level surface was now flawed here and there by a tiny ripple that flashed an occasional reflected sparkle from the high moon.

"Queer!" Greatorex ejaculated, and shivered as if he were suddenly cold.

"But, after all, why queer, G.,?" Harrison expostulated, although there was still a note of uneasiness in his voice. "I—I mean, there are always, on the stillest night, these slight movements of the air. We happen to notice it because it's so particularly still."

"Uncannily still," Greatorex murmured.

"Oh! damn it, G.," Harrison expostulated; "if you're going to get superstitious about meteorological conditions...."

"It's no use pretending, Harrison," Greatorex returned. "There is something uncanny about this place to-night. I'm not a superstitious man, as you know, but I don't mind confessing that I've got the creeps." He shivered again, and then added, "Come along, let's get back to your familiar house. I've had enough of this."

Harrison's only reply at the moment was a grunt of annoyance, but after they had turned into the path between the yews he began to talk again. "Admitting," he said, "that my nerves, too, are a trifle on edge, what does that prove, unless it is that we still retain something of the emotional fear of the savage?"

"What a chap you are for proving things this evening," Greatorex returned. "That argument with Vernon has upset you."

"They lay such stress on all these subjective reactions," Harrison grumbled, evidently continuing his own line of thought. "A normal psychology...."

But at this point they came out of the plantation into the clear spaces of the meadow and were instantly hailed by Fell and Mrs. Greatorex, who came forward to meet them.

"The others have gone on," Fell explained. "Lady Ulrica had a kind of faint, and Mrs. Harrison and Vernon have taken her back to the house. What a time you've been!"

"I suppose you didn't find anyone?" Mrs. Greatorex asked.

"No, no, we didn't," Harrison replied. "Only a part of the lady's apparel." And he exhibited the tulle scarf with the air of one prepared to explain a conjuring trick.

"Where did you find it?" Fell asked.

"On Harrison's back," Greatorex said.

"On his back?" ejaculated Fell.

"Simple enough, simple enough," Harrison explained. "We'd been dodging and skirmishing about the plantation, and, no doubt, I unknowingly scraped the thing off one of the trees. Greatorex saw it when we came out into the light by the lake."

"Yes," Greatorex commented, "and it was spread out over his coat as neatly as you please   might have been arranged there as a kind of joke."

"Herbert!" his wife ejaculated. "Do you mean that the woman was playing tricks on you; behind your back, as it were?"

Harrison clicked his tongue, as if he were facetiously reproving a child.

"Not you too, Mrs. Greatorex," he said. "I—I give you credit for more sense. The truth is that your good husband has brought with him into this life some of the old fears and superstitions that used to rule him when he plundered and murdered on the high seas. Yes—yes—in effect that's the truth, though we may find a biological explanation for the phenomenon without accepting any theory of reincarnation. It's—it's a case of latent cell memory, and to-night it has come out very—very strongly. He can find no explanation but the supernatural. I—I assure you, when a little bit of a breeze sprang up just now and set the poplars whispering, he was absolutely terrified. It only needed another touch to set him crossing himself and calling on his patron saint."

"Oh, Herbert!" Mrs. Greatorex expostulated. "You don't really believe it was a spirit, do you?"

Everyone knew that Greatorex had married beneath him, but his wife's usual method in company was to maintain a thoughtful silence that covered a multitude of faults. That method was one of her own devising. Her husband had never attempted to correct her. Nor did he now show the least impatience either with her unusual loquacity or her failure to appreciate Harrison's persiflage.

"No, my dear, as a matter of fact, I don't," he said; "but if you ask me, our host is almost painfully anxious to prove that the strange lady was of like substance to ourselves, of very flesh and bone subsisting; I forget just how the quotation goes."

"Well, of course she was," his wife replied with an air of assurance. "What else could she be?"

"Er—er—by the way, Mrs. Greatorex," Harrison put in. "Did you—er—see her plainly? Could you by any chance describe her for—for the purposes of identification?"

"Yes, I think I could," Mrs. Greatorex said cheerfully. "She was wearing a rather dowdy—old-fashioned, at least—white dress, more like a négligée than anything. I thought it funny she should come out in the garden in a thing like that. But I didn't make out quite what the material was. It looked like a rather fine linen tulle worn over a white linen petticoat, I thought. And she had a common scarf—but of course you've got that in your hand now...."

"Hm! yes," Harrison interrupted. "But her face, eh? Did you happen to catch her in profile, by any chance?"

"I don't know that I did notice her face very particularly," Mrs. Greatorex said. "She seemed quite an ordinary sort of young woman, I thought."

They had been retracing their way across the field as they talked, and now having reached the sunk fence, filed up the little flight of stone steps to the garden. Before them, across the width of the lawn the lighted windows of the drawing-room shone artificially yellow against the whiteness of the moonlight. They had returned to the influences of their own world; even the garden planned and formalised was a man-made thing. But as they crossed the short, well-kept turf, some common impulse made them pause, and with a movement that seemed to be concerted, turn back to look down over the meadow to the plantation and the solemn stretches of the lake—back to that other world, vague, mysterious and enormously still, into which they had so carelessly penetrated.

No one spoke until Harrison, with an impatient sigh, remarked suddenly: "Oh, come along! let's get back to sanity."

"Hm! Yes," Greatorex agreed.

"About time we went to bed," Harrison went on. "We'll be wiser in the morning."

"I suppose," Fell began as they resumed their walk to the house, but Harrison cut short his speculations.

"Here's Emma coming to reprove us," he interrupted. "She'll probably insist on our all taking something hot to ward off the evil effects of miasma."

Mrs. Harrison was, in fact, coming quickly to meet them with a brisk air of urgency, and as though she would shorten the little distance that still divided them, she called to her husband while she was still some few yards away, on a note that held the suggestion of a faint asperity.

"Charles. I want to speak to you," she said.

"Are we in the way?" Fell asked as they hurried to meet her.

Mrs. Harrison looked at him for a moment as if she had been unexpectedly reminded of the fact of his existence, and then, taking no notice of his question, continued:

"That man Messenger, from the hotel, is here, Charles, with the police sergeant. They want to see you at once."

Harrison's quick mind leapt at once to a possible explanation.

"Ha! Now we shall hear something about the lady of the lake, no doubt," he said.

"It's about Messenger's daughter," Mrs. Harrison replied. "She's—she has disappeared. They are looking for her; and Messenger wants to know if they can go down to the plantation. He has apparently got some idea that she may be there."

"Oh!" commented Harrison on a falling note, and exchanged a glance of understanding with his wife. Then they both turned and looked at Fell.

He had almost forgotten the resolutions he had made an hour earlier, and was quite unprepared to meet the silent accusation that was now levelled at him.

"I—I don't know anything about it," he stammered.

"Oh, well," Harrison said. "Let's go and hear what Messenger and the Sergeant have to tell us. I suppose this means that we shall have to make another pilgrimage to the lake."

Greatorex, in the rear of the procession, was heard to remark that he was damned if he could make head or tail of it.

PART 3: THE EXPLANATION

1

Mr. Messenger and the Sergeant were in the drawing-room talking to Lady Ulrica and Vernon, when Harrison, at the head of the little party, entered by the French window.

Mr. Messenger's story was soon told. His daughter had left the hotel presumably between nine and ten o'clock, and had not been seen since. He explained that he was peculiarly anxious because she had been in very low spirits recently. For one thing, a friend of hers, a Mrs. Burton who lived a few miles away, had committed suicide about three weeks before. Also, and here Mr. Messenger looked rather pointedly in the direction of Robert Fell; also, he believed that she had—he paused with obvious intention before he concluded—"she had—another trouble on her mind."

Harrison had listened with a preoccupied air that was unusual to him. But as the hotel-keeper finished his story, he warmed again to his usual alertness.

"I must tell you, Messenger," he said, "that we have only this moment come up from the lake, all of us. And we saw no sign of your daughter there, but we did meet another young woman, a perfect stranger to all of us, who behaved in—er—in a rather odd manner. Might I ask you if you have anyone staying with you who at all answers that description?"

"We've no one staying in the house at all this week-end, sir," Messenger replied.

"And do you know of anyone, any stranger staying in the village?"

"There's no one, sir, to my knowledge," Messenger said, and went on quickly: "But have I your permission now, sir, for me and Mr. Stevens to go down to the plantation, and—and the lake?" He paused before he added in a lower tone, "Though I'm afraid we'll be too late. She's been gone, now, for more than three hours."

"But we've just come back from the plantation, all of us," Harrison protested. "If she'd been there, surely we should have seen her?"

"Not if she'd ... if she'd been...." Messenger began, and stopped abruptly, putting his hand to his throat as if his words had choked him.

Stevens, the police-sergeant, shifted his feet uneasily and looked half-appealingly at Mrs. Harrison. "Mr. Messenger is afraid as Miss Phyllis may 'ave—may 'ave done what her friend Mrs. Burton did," he explained.

Mrs. Harrison got to her feet with a sudden effect of tense emotion, but before she could speak her husband cut in quickly by saying, "We'd better have the electric torches, Emma. Will you get them? G. and I will go, too. Will you come, Vernon?"

"Certainly," Vernon said. There was a light in his eyes that was hardly indicative of horror or even of pity.

Harrison turned away from him with a movement of disgust. "And Fell? Where's Fell?" he asked.

But Fell had already left the room.

"He went out by the window, a couple of minutes back, sir," the Sergeant said.

Charles Harrison was at all times an impatient man, and there were occasions, as in the present case, when his nervous irritability completely overcame him. He was seriously distressed by the thought that Phyllis Messenger had in all probability committed suicide. That touched him on his human, generous side. But the thing that had finally upset him had been the look on Vernon's face; rapt, faintly mystical, the look of one who believed that a very miracle had been performed for his benefit. Harrison could not endure to remain in his presence for another moment.

"I'll—I'll go on and see what's become of Fell," he mumbled as he fairly scuttled out of the room.

Once outside, he began to run. He wanted to think, but his mind was full of exasperation—with Vernon for his look of triumph, with the unfortunate Phyllis Messenger, with the vacillating Robert Fell as the immediate cause of the whole disaster. It seemed to Charles Harrison as if a fortuitous coincidence of events were conspiring against him to produce the illusion of a spiritualistic phenomenon. He did not believe for one moment that the stranger he had seen by the plantation was the spirit of the drowned Phyllis Messenger, but he foresaw the kind of case that Vernon would make out, and the effect it would have upon all the other members of the party. He could not even be sure that his own wife might not be influenced. When that confounded Stevens had hinted at the probability of this girl's suicide, a very queer expression had come into Emma's face, just as if she had suddenly realised some strange, significant connection between the possibility of the girl's death and that other experience earlier in the evening. He had cut hurriedly into the conversation for fear that she might say something foolish....

No, no, the girl could not, must not be dead. They would find her somewhere. And yet, so great was Harrison's foreboding that he never paused a moment by the yews, but hurried straight on to the shore of the lake. He had seen nothing of Fell. He had indeed forgotten all about him.

The night was still clear, but it was no longer frozen into that rigid immobility which had earlier produced so strange an effect of expectancy. There was a perceptible movement of air from the west, the familiar voices of the poplars maintained a perpetual background of sound, and when he had come through the plantation to the edge of the lake, he could hear the minute clashing of the reeds as the chasing ripple of the water set them gently swaying. The air of mystery had fled. He no longer felt the least influence of fear. The dread that he might presently see something that heavily floated, rocking and pressing against the rushes, was more the dread of annoyance.

But there was no one in sight. Nothing moved on all the long curving reaches of the bank. There was no sound in the night other than the faint crash of the reeds, the soft chuckle of the water and the steady insistence of the sibilant poplars.

And search as he would up and down the brooding sweep of the dark water, damascened here and there by the yellow silver of moonlight reflected from the crest of the increasing ripple, he could see no slender raft of floating drapery, nor any sign of a sodden form, nearly immersed, sagging inertly towards the bank.

He desisted presently, and sat down to consider the whole situation. The sense of exasperation had faded under the influence of the night's peace, and he fell into a calmer consideration of the problem that was vexing him. He saw that he must take the initiative, state his case before Vernon could get a word in. He would treat the affair as an instance of the kind of thing that gets worked up into what these people absurdly called "evidence." The coincidence of this stranger, (whoever she was,) turning up on the very evening on which that unhappy girl had drowned herself—if she had sunk, they would have an awful job to recover the body; the lake was over forty feet deep in places—was just another of those coincidences that had probably been responsible for most of the superstitions about the appearance of the spirit at the moment of death. And in this case it was obviously absurd to argue that it was the spirit of Phyllis Messenger they had seen. And heard! That was a good point. Finally and conclusively, there was the tulle scarf; real and solid enough. No one had ever heard of a spirit leaving such material evidence behind it. What had he done with that scarf, by the way? He had had it in his hand when he had entered the drawing-room. He'd probably laid it down there, somewhere. He must make enquiries about that as soon as he got in. It might help him to trace the identity of the stranger.

He had wandered a quarter of a mile or so away from the path through the plantation, and he jumped up now, with the intention of getting back at once to the house, in order to make sure of that valuable piece of evidence. But as he came out of his preoccupation, his attention was arrested by the distant murmur of little detached sounds, the separated notes of human voices, musical in their remoteness, faintly impinging upon the textured whisperings of the night.

They are still looking for that poor girl, he thought with a twinge of remorse for his own loss of interest in the search. But even as he started to join them, he realised that the sounds were retreating, fading imperceptibly into the depths of the night. Have they found her, I wonder, he murmured to himself, thinking still of a desecrated and draggled body; and then he heard himself being distantly hailed in the strong, cheerful voice of his friend Greatorex.

"Ahoy there, Harrison; Harrison, ahoy!" he was shouting.

It was not in the least the voice one would expect from a man who had so recently stood in the presence of the dead.

"Ahoy! Hallo! Where are you?" Harrison shouted in return.

The next minute he saw the tall, athletic figure of Greatorex coming towards him along the bank of the lake.

"Been looking for you everywhere," Greatorex said as he came within speaking distance. "We've found the lady."

"Alive?" gasped Harrison.

"Rather. Not exactly hearty, perhaps, but she's all right. Well enough, in any case, to walk back to the house in the company of her father and Fell." He dropped his voice confidentially as he added: "Seems that it's a case with Fell. What? We found 'em together, you know, in a cosy little place among the yews, not five yards from the spot where the mysterious lady came out. Perfect little tunnel up to it, too. If we'd happened on it at first, we'd have found the girl there and saved all the trouble. Fell knew all about the place, it seems. Went straight to it and found Miss Messenger in a faint, or just recovering from it."

"How long had she been there?" Harrison asked sharply.

"All the time, presumably," Greatorex said.

"Come there to meet Fell, eh?"

"Seems probable. And we spoilt his little game by coming too, I suppose. However, he's owned up now. Made a clean breast of it, and declared his intention of marrying her; in the presence of five witnesses. Quite a dramatic little scene there was. Old Messenger was almost overcome."

Harrison did not seem to have been attending to this speech, for his next question was:

"You didn't find anything else there, did you? No apparatus of any kind, such as a mask or attempts at a disguise?"

"Lord, no. I didn't see anything, and I was the first to get to them," Greatorex replied. "But why? You don't think...."

"That she may have been prepared? I do," Harrison said emphatically. "She'd made an assignation and come ready to pass herself off as someone else if she were caught—which she very nearly was. Showed herself in the first instance in order to attract Fell's attention, and unfortunately for her brought the whole party out."

"Oh! no, no, Harrison. No, I don't think so," Greatorex said. "You've got that blessed apparition or whatever it was on your nerves. But, honestly, that explanation won't do. Why, the girl was half-unconscious when I found 'em."

"Put on," Harrison interpolated.

"Impossible," Greatorex replied. "When we got her out into the open, she was still as white as a sheet."

"Effect of moonlight," commented Harrison.

"No." Greatorex's tone had a quality of great assurance. "No, she was recovering from a faint all right. There can be no question of that. Besides, what could be the point of all that make-believe after she was found?"

"Well, she may have fainted after she'd fooled us," Harrison suggested. "Overwrought, you know."

They had been making their way steadily back to the house as they talked, but Greatorex stopped now in the middle of the meadow, and took Harrison by the lapel of his dinner-jacket.

"Bad line, my friend," he said gravely. "Take my advice and don't attempt it before Vernon. I'm advising you for your good."

"Well, then, who the devil was it?" Harrison snapped impatiently.

"Ah! there you have me," Greatorex said.

"But, good God, G.," Harrison expostulated. "You don't believe that it was a—er—an apparition."

"Dunno what to think," Greatorex said.

Harrison blew a deep breath of disgust. "I thought you had more sense," he snapped out.

"Well, I'm willing to be convinced," Greatorex replied; "if you have any other explanation to offer."

But Harrison had nothing further to say in the matter just then. He wanted to see Phyllis Messenger first, alone. When he had got his evidence, he would be ready to offer his explanation.

They found only Mrs. Harrison and Mrs. Greatorex in the drawing-room when they entered by the French window. Messenger, his daughter, Stevens and Fell had gone back to the hotel, she explained, and Vernon and Lady Ulrica were in the morning-room, conferring, so Mrs. Harrison suggested, over the events of the evening.

"I don't quite know whether Mr. Fell means to come back," Mrs. Harrison concluded with a lift of her eyebrows. "He seemed—well, rather ashamed of himself altogether. I'm not sure that he hasn't taken his things."

"Just as well, perhaps," her husband said. And then his observant glance fell on the tulle scarf thrown over the back of a chair.

"Did you find out whom that belonged to?" he asked sharply.

"Oh!" ejaculated Mrs. Harrison. "They left it behind after all. It's Miss Messenger's. She identified it at once and wondered how it had got here."

"Certain it was hers, I suppose?" Harrison asked.

"Oh yes! It's got her initials worked on it," his wife told him.

For a few seconds Harrison stood thoughtfully drawing the scarf through his hands, then dropping it back on to the chair, he said: "That's all right, then. Hadn't we better be going to bed? It's after one o'clock."

II

When Charles Harrison set about the investigation of that night's mystery, he was still intent upon the theory that the appearance he had seen and spoken to was in fact the living personality of some stranger who had been staying either in the village or possibly at Orton Park, the grounds of which sloped down to the other side of the lake. There were a couple of canoes and a punt in Lord Orton's boathouse, and the crossing presented no real difficulty. He was, however, finally deflected from that theory in the course of his interview with Miss Messenger.

He had been quite firm at breakfast. As a result, no doubt, of the "conference" they had held the night before, Lady Ulrica and Vernon were eager to begin an immediate discussion of what they called the "phenomenon." Harrison effectively stopped that.

"No! no!! no!!!" he said, putting his hands over his ears as soon as the topic was opened. "Now, Vernon, you profess to be scientific in your investigations. You—you insisted on that in your—er—lecture under the cedar last night. Now listen to me. I promise to thrash this out with you—presently. To—to discuss the thing in all its bearings. But I at least mean to be thorough and careful in my methods. Give me to-day to examine the case. I must cross-examine the principal witness—er—alone. Yes. I insist on that. You'll have the very best intentions, of course. I don't doubt it. But you'll offer suggestions—unconsciously, perhaps, but you'll do it."

"And you?" Vernon replied. "Won't you put suggestions into the examinee's mind, too?"

"Hm! hm! You'll have to trust me," Harrison said. "I assure you that I only want to arrive at the truth of—of the actual facts, you understand. I want to know what Miss Messenger was doing down there for three hours or more. And if you want me to discuss the thing with you, you must let me get at the facts in my own way. I—I make that a condition. If you won't agree to it, I shall refuse to discuss the thing at all."

"Oh, very well," Vernon agreed.

And Harrison had gone off to the hotel after breakfast, in the cheerful state of mind of one who has good reasons to hope for the best.

Miss Messenger received him in the private parlour of the hotel, a room that evidenced her desperate efforts to alleviate the influence of the original furniture.

She professed to be completely recovered from the effects of her adventure, and indeed she displayed no sign of illness. Her engagement to Robert Fell was, it seemed, an understood thing, and she received Mr. Harrison's congratulations with the air proper to the occasion. Harrison, who had only known her very slightly hitherto, decided in his own mind that she was a very charming young woman, and came at last to the purpose of his visit with a slight effect of apology.

"I—I don't know whether you have heard, Miss Messenger," he began, "that we had another visitor in the plantation last night."

She opened her eyes at that, with a genuine surprise that could not be mistaken.

"Didn't Mr. Fell or your father say anything to you about it?" Harrison continued.

She looked at him with obvious perplexity. "About another visitor?" she repeated. "No, they haven't told me anything. I don't quite understand."

"I—I'll explain in a moment," Harrison said. "There are just one or two little questions that I'd like to ask you first, if you don't mind?"

She shook her head with a sigh. "No, I don't mind," she said. "I suppose as a matter of fact you know all about it already?"

"Something," Harrison agreed, shrewdly guessing at her meaning. "So far as you and Mr. Fell are concerned at least. But—well—I'll tell you in a moment why I want to know—could you say what the time was when you got to the plantation?"

"A little before ten," she told him. "I heard the stable clock in Orton Park strike after I'd been there a few minutes."

"Hm! hm! And what did you do exactly between ten o'clock and—er—half-past twelve or so?" Harrison enquired.

Phyllis Messenger's face glowed suddenly red. "I—I don't know," she said after a marked pause.

"Did you go to sleep, for instance?" Harrison asked with a friendly smile.

She shook her head. "It wasn't a sleep," she said, and then went on quickly: "Oh, you said you knew—something. Don't you know how—how unhappy I was?"

Mr. Harrison turned his head away and stared at the ferns in the fireplace. "I've heard something," he murmured.

"About my friend Rhoda Burton?" Miss Messenger said.

"Ah! yes. She—she committed suicide about a month ago, I believe?" Harrison mumbled.

"Well, I meant to do that, too," Phyllis Messenger burst out with a sudden boldness. "In there, where they found me. I meant to—to strangle myself with my tulle scarf. I tied it round my neck and I meant to do it. And then I couldn't."

"Yes?" Harrison prompted her gently.

"Oh, and then I threw it down—the scarf, I mean—and everything went black. I thought I was going to die. I went down on my knees and tried to pray. I don't remember anything after that until—until they found me."

Harrison's agile mind seized the significance of this evidence in a flash. At one stroke it eliminated the probability of that scarf having been worn by a stranger. If the scarf had lain there by the side of the swooning Miss Messenger, no one but a mad woman could have callously picked it up, worn it and postured before a group of half a dozen people without making the least mention of the helpless figure to whom it belonged. For a moment he played with the thought of a madwoman, but dismissed it. If there was a madwoman in Long Orton or the neighbourhood, he would have heard of her.

He sighed heavily, and chiefly for the sake of giving himself more time, said, "You're quite sure you had the scarf with you?"

"Well, of course," Miss Messenger replied. "I only bought it last week;" and added with a shudder, "but I don't ever want to see it again." There could be no question of the vividness of the unhappy memories associated in her mind with that particular article of apparel.

"It doesn't follow, however," Harrison went on thoughtfully after a perceptible pause, "that because you have no memory of anything after you fainted, you never moved from the spot where you were found?"

Miss Messenger shrugged her shoulders. "I can't say anything about that, can I?" she asked.

"You see," Harrison explained, "earlier in the evening, it may have been about eleven or thereabouts, my friends and I saw someone down by the plantation, and—and went down to investigate. And there we met and spoke to—er—someone who was unquestionably wearing your scarf—which she later discarded. It was found later by myself, as a matter of fact."

"How very extraordinary!" was all Miss Messenger's comment. Her surprise and interest, however, were beyond question.

"Inexplicable," Harrison agreed.

"But who could it have been?" Miss Messenger besought him.

"It could, so far as I can make out, only have been yourself—in a trance," Harrison replied. He instinctively disliked the sound of that last word, but could find no other. People who have "swooned" or fainted do not walk about in that condition. "Er—you've never, I suppose—er—been in that state of unconsciousness before?" he went on quickly, as if to obliterate the effect of the too suggestive word.

"Not actually," Miss Messenger said, hesitated, and then continued: "but I've—felt queer once or twice lately."

"Queer?" Harrison prompted her.

"As if—as if I were going off like I did last night," she explained. "Only lately, though. Only since my friend died."

"Mrs. Burton?"

She nodded.

"Hm. Very sad, very," said Harrison, getting up, and then he added: "It was very good of you to answer my questions, and I think, now, that I am satisfied as to the identity of the stranger. You must have walked in your trance last night, Miss Messenger, and made your way back again to the place where we found you, dropping your scarf on the way. You must forgive us for not recognising you in the half-light."

Miss Messenger had no comment to make on that explanation. It was evident that she was not in a position to deny his statement, even if she had had the desire to do so....

And after that interview, Harrison began to see his way quite clearly. When he left the hotel he visited the scene of last night's encounter in order to make a thorough examination of the place itself, and especially of that curious little enceinte among the yews where Miss Messenger had been found. He thought it possible that he might discover fresh evidence.

No fresh evidence, however, rewarded his investigation.

III

He was, nevertheless, in very good spirits at dinner that night. The discussion had been postponed by common consent until the evening, but he once or twice referred to it in the course of the meal.

Greatorex, noting his host's almost gleeful manner, asked him if he had got new and conclusive evidence in the process of his investigations, but Harrison refused to answer that.

"No, no," he said. "We'll have it out after dinner. Vernon has got his case, and I have mine. We'll argue, and then put it to the vote. Do you agree, Vernon?"

Vernon, no less confident than his antagonist, agreed willingly enough, and later, when they were all gathered together in the drawing-room, he agreed also to open the discussion.

"It's all so clear to me," he said. "I cannot see how there can be two opinions."

"Well, fire away," Harrison encouraged him.

Vernon leaned back in his chair, and clasped his hands behind his head.

"I postulate to begin with," he said, "that we were all in precisely the right, expectant, slightly inert condition necessary to the production of phenomena. We were sitting in a circle, and our conscious minds were completely occupied with the subject of spiritualism. We were, in fact, according to the common agreement about such things, in the state that best enables us to assist any possible manifestations by—by giving out power.

"The chief medium in the case was unquestionably the unconscious person of Miss Messenger. She was in what I may call an ideal trance for the purpose of manifestation. Also, by an extraordinary chance, her body was secluded and in darkness. If the conditions had been planned by experts they could hardly have been improved upon. After that our explanation of the apparition and of the 'direct voice' phenomena is largely dependent upon precedents.

"With regard to the first, I claim that von Schrenck-Notsing's photographs taken in Paris and elsewhere in 1912 and 1913 have sufficiently demonstrated that in favourable conditions and with a sensitive medium, a form of matter, not as yet scientifically described, may be drawn from the body of the medium and used by the external agency to build up representations not only of the human form, but also of familiar materials. I mention that in order that we may not be in any way disturbed by the fact that the materialisation was dressed in a gown of different colour from that worn by Miss Messenger. That gown too was instantly woven out of the creative flux.

"Indeed, the only thing that was not so momentarily created and re-absorbed was the tulle scarf. That must actually have been taken from Miss Messenger's unconscious body and handled by the temporary form evolved out of the teleplasm. There is good precedent for that, as I believe I said last night."

He paused a moment and then, as Harrison did not immediately reply, he added: "And if we are all agreed, after we have finished our discussion this evening, I would like to have separate written accounts from each of you as to your sight of the phenomenon; those, backed by the evidence of Mr. Messenger, his daughter and the police sergeant, ought, I think, to establish one of the most remarkable and convincing cases ever reported to the S.P.R."

"Steady, steady, Vernon," Harrison put in. "I can't say that I'm absolutely convinced as yet."

"What's the alternative explanation?" Vernon asked.

"That it was Miss Messenger herself whom we saw in a state of trance," Harrison said. "You see I concede you the trance."

"But, my dear man," Vernon expostulated, "the figure we saw by the wood was not like Miss Messenger."

"No?" Harrison replied. "Very well, let's analyse the differences as observed by the various witnesses. You begin, Vernon. Was there any difference in height?"

"None to speak of that I noticed," Vernon admitted, "but that woman had a distinctly more spiritual face than Miss Messenger."

"Anything else?" Harrison pressed him.

"We only saw her for a few moments, of course," Vernon said. "I must confess that at the moment I can't think of any other marked differences. It—it was another face and expression, that's all."

"And you, Emma," said Harrison, looking at his wife.

"I couldn't be absolutely sure that it wasn't Miss Messenger," she replied. "We were all in rather an excited state just then, weren't we?"

"But the dress was a different colour," put in Mrs. Greatorex. "That first woman was in white. Miss Messenger had a grey dress on."

"I think, you know," her husband continued, "that Vernon rather hit the mark when he said that the first girl had a more spiritual face. That was what struck me."

"Haven't you any comments, Lady Ulrica?" Harrison asked.

Lady Ulrica sighed. "I'm afraid," she said honestly, "that for observations of that kind, you can't count on me one way or the other. I'd left my glasses under the cedar, and I'm as blind as a bat without them."

Harrison smiled and shrugged his shoulders. "Well, come, what does it all amount to?" he asked. "Is there any reason in the world why we should resort to so far-fetched an explanation as the supernatural? Let us consider the evidence as if we were going to put it before a body of expert opinion. We were, according to Vernon's own admission, in an 'expectant, slightly inert condition.' We had been talking spiritualism for an hour or more after dinner, in very exceptional conditions. I never remember a stiller or an—er—more emotional night. When we were all worked up by Vernon's eloquence into a peculiar state of anticipation, we saw a white figure down by the lake. It was inevitable, in these circumstances, that we should approach it in a state of emotion. And what did we find? We found a young woman walking in trance. Well, that state had very naturally altered her usual appearance, given her face a more spiritual expression. No doubt, she was very pale. She told me this morning that she had contemplated suicide just before she fell into this trance, and I conceive it as being probable that her highly disturbed mental condition had reacted upon her physical appearance.

"Now let us consider what actually happened. Three observers, Emma, Fell and myself, had seen Miss Messenger before and failed in those circumstances to recognise her. Is that a very remarkable failure when we give due weight to our own excited anticipations, coupled with the fact that the girl was in an altogether abnormal physical state? Furthermore we find that four people fail later to recognise Miss Messenger as the original of the supposed stranger. Of these four, one admits that she cannot be trusted as an observer of the details, another that she hardly noticed the stranger's face. A third, Vernon, cannot deny that he was the victim of a prepossession, that he anticipated a spiritualistic phenomenon and he is not therefore a reliable witness. The fourth is our friend Greatorex. Now, G., I ask you in all seriousness whether you would be prepared to swear on oath that the figure we saw for a few seconds in the moonlight down by the yews could not have been Miss Messenger in a state of trance. On your oath, now."

"No, Harrison, no. I would not be prepared to swear that," Greatorex said. "In fact, I believe you're right about the whole affair."

"But the dress, Mr. Harrison," Mrs. Greatorex put in. "That woman by the wood was in white. Miss Messenger was wearing a grey dress."

"The effect of moonlight, my dear lady," Harrison replied. "Moonlight takes the colour out of everything." As he spoke, he got to his feet and took a turn up the room. As he had argued, the conviction of the truth of his theory had been steadily growing in his own mind. He wanted, now, to clinch the thing once and for all, eliminate the last possibility of sending in a report to the S. P. R., and lay the ghost for ever. But as he reached the end of the room, his eye fell on the tulle scarf left by Miss Messenger on the previous night, now neatly folded by the housemaid and laid on a table by the window. And he realised in an instant that the confounded thing was grey and matched the colour of Miss Messenger's dress. Why then had that scarf also not appeared white in the moonlight? It meant nothing; no doubt he might be able to evolve some explanation, but at the present moment it might most vexatiously complicate his case. Everyone, strangely enough, had recognised that scarf. It was the one thing that had appeared to be unaltered by the unusual conditions.

Harrison was intellectually honest, but the temptation to suppress that piece of evidence was too strong for him. As he turned, he was between the table and the rest of the party, and he stretched his hand out behind him, and surreptitiously crammed the scarf into the pocket of his dinner-jacket.

But his peroration was spoilt. The enthusiasm seemed to have been suddenly drained out of him.

"Hm! hm! Well, in effect," he said as he returned, "I submit that there is no reason whatever to seek a supernatural explanation of our experience last night. What do you all say?"

"Personally, I'm quite convinced that it was Miss Messenger we saw," his wife replied cheerfully.

"Very probably, I should say," Greatorex agreed.

"It certainly seems the most likely explanation," Mrs. Greatorex added.

"And you, Lady Ulrica?" Harrison asked.

"Well, of course, if you are all sure it was Miss Messenger, I don't see that there's anything more to be said," Lady Ulrica replied.

"All of us except Vernon," Harrison amended.

Vernon sighed and leaned back in his chair. "You've pretty effectively diddled my report to the S.P.R., anyway," he said. "If no one is prepared to swear that the person we first saw was not Miss Messenger, I've got no evidence."

"There is still Fell, of course," Harrison suggested.

"I don't think we can rely upon anything Mr. Fell might say," Mrs. Harrison put in. "I'm afraid he had a reason for not wanting to recognise Miss Messenger just then. I don't think Mr. Fell has behaved at all nicely."

"I think we'll drop it, Harrison," Vernon said with a touch of magnanimity. "I can't say that you've convinced me, even about last night's experience, but you've got all the ordinary probabilities on your side. It's curious how difficult it is even to plan a perfect test case."

IV

Harrison had triumphed. He ought to have been content. But the truth is that he had satisfied everyone but himself. "That confounded scarf," as he began to think of it, bothered and perplexed him. He stowed it away in a drawer when he went to bed, but in the small hours of the morning he found himself wide awake reconsidering all the evidence. It had come to him with a perfectly detestable clearness that if Vernon's theory was a true one, that scarf was the single piece of common earthly material that had been used in the presentation of the phenomenon they had witnessed; and it was, at least, a strangely significant fact that the scarf should be the one thing they had all seen so clearly, the one thing the appearance of which had not been influenced by their mental emotion or the effect of moonlight.

The coincidence bothered him. He could not find an explanation.

It continued to bother him the next morning. It came between him and his work. And after lunch he put the scarf in his pocket and made it an excuse to call again on Miss Messenger. There were, perhaps, one or two further points that might be elucidated in conversation with her. She had taken, he judged, almost as violent an antipathy to the thing as he had himself. The sight of it might produce some kind of shock, might just possibly revive some memory of what had happened during her trance.

When he arrived at the hotel, Miss Messenger was in the garden, and he was shown up into her private sitting-room to await her. Still thoughtfully considering the best means to approach the production of the scarf, he walked absent-mindedly across the room and began to stare at the photographs on the mantelpiece. And then, suddenly, he became aware of the illusion that he was gazing at a background of dark yews, against which was vividly posed the delicate profile of some exquisite cameo. He blinked his eyes in amazement, and the background changed to the commonplace detail reflected in the mirror. But the face remained, the very profile he had seen by the plantation, a face sensitive and full of sadness, staring wistfully out as if at some unwelcome vision of the future.

Harrison shivered. It seemed to him as if a thin draught of cold air were blowing past him. And then, for a moment, he had a sense of immense distances and strange activities beyond the knowledge of common life. He was aware of some old experience newly recognised after long ages of forgetfulness; an experience that came back to him elusive as the thought of a recent dream. But while he struggled to place that fugitive memory, the door behind him opened, and the dark curtain of physical reality was suddenly interposed between him and his vision.

He heard the voice of Miss Messenger speaking to him close at hand.

"That's my friend, Rhoda Burton," she was saying. "The photograph was taken only a week before she died. She was in great trouble even then, poor darling."

John Davys Beresford – A Concise Bibliography

The Early History of Jacob Stahl (1911), the first of a trilogy A Candidate for Truth and The Invisible Event
The Hampdenshire Wonder (1911) Novel
A Candidate for Truth (1912)
Goslings: A World of Women (1913) Novel
The House in Demetrius Road (1914) Novel
The Invisible Event (1915) Novel
H.G. Wells (1915) Criticism
These Lynneskers (1916) Novel
William Elphinstone Ford (1917) Biography, with Kenneth Richmond

House Mates (1917) Novel
Nineteen Impressions (1918) Stories
God's Counterpoint (1918) Novel
The Jervaise Comedy (1919) Novel
The Imperfect Mother (1920) Novel
Signs and Wonders (1921) Stories
Revolution (1921) Novel
The Prisoner of Hartling (1922) Novel
The Imperturbable Duchess & Other Stories (1923)
Monkey Puzzle (1925)
That Kind of Man, or Almost Pagan (1926) Novel
The Decoy (1927) Novel
The Instrument of Destiny (1928) A mystery novel
All or Nothing (1928) Novel
Real People (1929) Novel
The Meeting Place and Other Stories (1929)
Love's Illusion (1930)
The Next Generation (1932) Novel
The Old People (1932) Novel
The Camberwell Miracle (1933) Novel
Peckover (1934) Novel
On a Huge Hill (1935) Novel
Blackthorn Winter & Other Stories (1936)
Cleo (1937) Novel
What Dreams May Come (1941) Novel
A Common Enemy (1941) Novel
Men in the Same Boat (1943) (with Esmé Wynne-Tyson)
The Riddle of the Tower (1944) (with Esme Wynne-Tyson)
The Gift (1947) (with Esme Wynne-Tyson)
The Prisoner
Love's Pilgrim